Concord Theatricals Acting Edition

C000254364

Everyl Talking About Jamie

Teen Edition

Book & Lyrics by
Tom MacRae

Music by
Dan Gillespie Sells

From an idea by
Jonathan Butterell

concord
theatricals

FOR PRODUCTION INQUIRIES

UNITED STATES AND CANADA
info@concordtheatricals.com
1-866-979-0447

UNITED KINGDOM AND EUROPE
licensing@concordtheatricals.co.uk
020-7054-7298

Each title is subject to availability from Concord Theatricals Corp.,
depending upon country of performance. Please be aware that
EVERYBODY'S TALKING ABOUT JAMIE: TEEN EDITION may not
be licensed by Concord Theatricals Corp. in your territory. Professional
and amateur producers should contact the nearest Concord Theatricals
Corp. office or licensing partner to verify availability.

This work is published by Concord Theatricals Corp.

No one shall make any changes in this title(s) for the purpose of production. No part of this book may be reproduced, stored in a retrieval system, scanned, uploaded, or transmitted in any form, by any means, now known or yet to be invented, including mechanical, electronic, digital, photocopying, recording, videotaping, or otherwise, without the prior written permission of the publisher. No one shall share this title(s), or any part of this title(s), through any social media or file hosting websites.

For all inquiries regarding motion picture, television, online/digital and other media rights, please contact Concord Theatricals Corp.

THIRD-PARTY MATERIALS USE NOTE

Licensees are solely responsible for obtaining formal written permission from copyright owners to use copyrighted third-party materials (e.g., incidental music not provided in connection with a performance license, artworks, logos) in the performance of this play and are strongly cautioned to do so. If no such permission is obtained by the licensee, then the licensee must use only original materials and materials that the licensee owns and controls. Licensees are solely responsible and liable for clearances of all third-party copyrighted materials, and shall indemnify the copyright owners of the play(s) and their licensing agent, Concord Theatricals Corp., against any costs, expenses, losses and liabilities arising from the use of such copyrighted third-party materials by licensees. For music, please contact the appropriate music licensing authority in your territory for the rights to any incidental music not provided in connection with a performance license.

IMPORTANT BILLING AND CREDIT REQUIREMENTS

If you have obtained performance rights to this title, please refer to your licensing agreement for important billing and credit requirements.

EVERYBODY'S TALKING ABOUT JAMIE was first produced by Sheffield Theatres at the Crucible Theatre on February 9, 2017 and was inspired by the BBC Three documentary *Jamie: Drag Queen At 16* produced by Firecracker Films and directed by Jenny Popplewell. The show transferred to the Apollo Theatre in London's West End, produced by Nica Burns and co-producers Ian Osborne, Paula Marie Black, Teresa and Craig Beech, on November 6, 2017. The performance was directed by Jonathan Butterell, with choreography by Kate Prince, set and costumes by Anna Fleischle, lighting by Lucy Carter, video design by Luke Halls, and sound by Paul Groothuis. The cast in the West End was as follows:

LAIKA VIRGIN.	Alex Anstey
RAY	Mina Anwar
DEAN PAXTON	Luke Baker
FATIMAH.	Courtney Bowman
MISS HEDGE	Tamsin Carroll
JAMIE'S DAD	Ken Christiansen
SAYID.	Jordan Cunningham
LEVI	Daniel Davids
TRAY SOPHISTICAY	James Gillan
MICKEY	Ryan Hughes
SANDRA BOLLOCK	Daniel Jacob
JAMIE NEW	John McCrea
HUGO	Phil Nichol
BEX	Harriet Payne
CY	Shiv Rabheru
BECCA	Lauran Rae
PRITTI PASHA	Lucie Shorthouse
VICKI	Kirstie Skivington
MARGARET NEW	Josie Walker
UNDERSTUDY	Rebecca McKinnis
SWINGS	Luke Bayer, Marvyn Charles, Cherelle Jay, Chloe Pole

EVERYBODY'S TALKING ABOUT JAMIE: TEEN EDITION was first produced by Notre Dame High School, Sheffield in Sheffield, South Yorkshire, England on December 7, 2021. The production was directed by Emma Carrigan, Paul O'Farrell, and Kathryn Corbett. The music team was Tom Owen, Katherine Prestwood, and Jon Mugridge. Choreography was by Sadie Webb.

CHARACTERS

MISS HEDGE – a teacher, thirties/forties

BECCA – a school pupil, Black

VICKI – a school pupil

CY – a school pupil, Asian

BEX – a school pupil, White

SAYID – a school pupil, Muslim

FATIMAH – a school pupil, Iranian

PRITTI – a school pupil, Muslim

DEAN PAXTON – a school pupil

LEVI – a school pupil, Black

MICKEY – a school pupil

JAMIE NEW – a school pupil, our hero

MARGARET NEW – Jamie's mother

RAY – Margaret's best friend

HUGO / LOCO CHANELLE – a faded former drag queen and his retired alter ego, forties/fifties

LAIKA VIRGIN – a drag queen

TRAY SOPHISTICAY – a drag queen

SANDRA BOLLOCK – a drag queen

YOUNG LOCO CHANELLE – Hugo's younger self

THE OTHER WOMAN – a woman from Hugo's past

JOHN – a man from Hugo's past

JAMIE'S DAD

LAD 1 – a local lad

LAD 2 – a local lad

LAD 3 – a local lad

NOTES ON CASTING

There is an **ENSEMBLE** that can be expanded to any size according to the needs of your production.

To reduce cast size, **TRAY SOPHISTICAY** can double as **YOUNG LOCO CHANELLE**, **SANDRA BOLLOCK** as **JOHN**, and **LAIKA VIRGIN** as **THE OTHER WOMAN**. One of the drag queens can also double for **JAMIE'S DAD**. **LADS 1, 2 & 3** can be played by three boys from among the school kids.

Licensees should use reasonable best efforts to cast the characters as written in the character descriptions, especially regarding race, gender, ethnicity, and religious identity. Please reach out to your licensing representative if you have any questions.

TIME & SETTING

Everybody's Talking About Jamie: Teen Edition is set around Parson Cross, a working class area of Sheffield in 2017.

AUTHORS' NOTES

THE KIDS:

Everybody's Talking About Jamie: Teen Edition is set in a world where kids do not go to the theatre, and have almost certainly never seen a stage musical. They are raucous, real and rough around the edges. They must never be too polished, too trained, too shiny and should never be played as an amorphous group. Every school kid has their own name, their own personality, their own story – and that should be reflected at every point in the production. Even in the group choreography, each individual character should shine through. In their dialogue and performance they each have their own full internal lives.

THE ADULTS:

Our characters are working-class Northerners. This means they keep their emotions close to their chest and do not easily become sentimental or romantic. They can be full of love – but it is always tough love, and any show of emotion has to be earned. When it is earned, it will be truly profound.

THE MUSIC:

Jamie's world is a pop music world. The characters sing as contemporary characters would sing in real life, reflecting the style of music that they listen to. Margaret loves Dusty Springfield. Jamie loves contemporary pop. Their vocal choices should reflect that. None of these characters know that they are in a musical, so should never sing, dance or act as such.

A NOTE ABOUT UNIFORM:

Unlike some parts of the world, where only private school students wear school uniform, nearly all British state schools (government-funded public schools) have a strict school uniform code. The fact that Jamie and his friends wear school uniform is not an indication that their school is smart, exclusive or wealthy. In fact, it is quite the opposite.

But most importantly...

Go and have fun! Maybe you are sixteen as you read this – and it's terrible and it's wonderful and it's frightening and it's exciting and it's the best of us and the worst of us all at the same time. So capture that, or recapture that, and go put that on stage.

MUSICAL NUMBERS

And You Don't Even Know It................... Jamie, Miss Hedge, Kids

The Wall in My Head.............................. Jamie, Ensemble

Spotlight... Pritti, Ensemble

Spotlight (Reprise) ....Jamie, Pritti, Ensemble

The Legend of Loco Chanelle.............. Hugo, Drag Queens, Ensemble

The Legend of Loco Chanelle (Reprise)...........................Hugo

If I Met Myself Again. .... Margaret

Work of Art. .... Miss Hedge, Dean, Jamie, Ensemble

Over the Top. .... Loco Chanelle, Drag Queens, Ensemble

Out of the Darkness. ....Off-Stage Ensemble

Everybody's Talking About Jamie. .... Company

Limited Edition. ....Ray, Jamie, Margaret, Ensemble

It Means Beautiful... Pritti

It Means Beautiful (Reprise)................................... Pritti

Ugly in This Ugly World ....Jamie, Male Ensemble

He's My Boy.. Margaret

And You Don't Even Know It (Bus Station Reprise)...........Jamie, Lad 1, Lad 2, Lad 3

My Man, Your Boy................................Jamie, Margaret

The Prom Song... Company

Finale...Company

Out of the Darkness (Encore)............................... Company

ACT I

1. Mayfield School: Classroom

(The blast of a school bell – and the stage comes to life.

[MUSIC NO. 00 'DON'T EVEN KNOW IT ENTRANCE']

We're looking at a tatty, ordinary classroom. Among the kids:)

*(**BEX** and **BECCA**, best friends, the pretty, popular girls, gobby but not too mean. **BEX** is white, **BECCA** is black.)*

*(**SAYID**, a Muslim boy.)*

*(**DEAN**, good-looking but a bit of a bully.)*

*(**PRITTI**, a plain-looking Muslim girl, headscarf, super-smart but very shy.)*

*(Other kids include **CY**, **FATIMAH**, **LEVI**, **MICKEY**, and **VICKI**.)*

*(Their teacher is **MISS HEDGE**, dark, business-smart clothes – but with very smart red high heels on, a little grace note of fabulousness.)*

MISS HEDGE. Calm it down Year Eleven! Year Eleven! YEAR Eleven!!! What did I just say?

BECCA. Dunno Miss, I couldn't hear, cos it's like *really* noisy in here.

MISS HEDGE. Becca!

BECCA. OI VICKI, WE STILL ON FOR FRIDAY OR WHAT?

MISS HEDGE. Becca!

VICKI. I need my brother though, or we can't get vodka.

MISS HEDGE. Vicki!

CY. You having a party? Can I come?

BECCA, VICKI & BEX. NO.

LEVI. Can I come?

BECCA, VICKI & BEX. YES.

LEVI. Boom!

MISS HEDGE. Cy! Becca! Bex! Vicki! Levi! All of you! BE QUIET!!!

> (**MISS HEDGE** *proper yells it – and the class goes silent.*)

> (*Beat. Then, as one, they give a sarcastic 'Oooooooooooh!'*)

SAYID. Miss, are you stressed?

FATIMAH. Aw bless her, she is too.

BEX. Miss, what have you got to be stressed about Miss?

BECCA. Yeah Miss, what have you got to be stressed about?

BEX. Are you getting stressed now?

BECCA. Is this stressing you now?

BEX. Are we stressing you?

MISS HEDGE. Just –

> (*Mimes 'zip it'.*)

Now, as I was saying, as this is your *final* careers lesson...

MICKEY. Woohoo!!!

> (**MISS HEDGE** *looks at the class – not a single student apart from* **PRITTI** *is listening. She sighs.*)

MISS HEDGE. Pritti, you've been paying attention, would you kindly explain to the rest of the class?

> (**PRITTI** *gets nervously to her feet.*)

PRITTI. Miss is saying that you can't all be like, pop singers and movie stars, that there's other jobs just like normal stuff and that – and they're kinda good too.

MISS HEDGE. Thank you Pritti! Having realistic expectations about your future career potential is what will eventually get you a real job. So what do you want to be?

PRITTI. A doctor Miss.

DEAN. As if!

> *(This gets laughs and hoots of derision from the class.)*

MISS HEDGE. Settle down Year Eleven! At least a doctor is a proper career, not *X Factor* reality TV rubbish. Pritti's got a dream, but she's prepared to work hard to be a doctor. And if not love you can always get a job at a vets. Or Boots.

> (**PRITTI** *sits down, grateful to be out of the spotlight.*)

Yes Bex?

BEX. Miss – why does she get to be a doctor, and I have to work in an abattoir?

MISS HEDGE. I'm sorry?

BEX. This careers brochure you gave me –

> (**BEX** *holds up a shiny brochure.*)

– 'Your Future In Meat'.

MISS HEDGE. Yes, well that was just a *suggestion* –

BEX. Is it because I'm white?

DEAN. Her! In an abattoir!

BECCA. Shut up Dean!

DEAN. Shut up Becca!

BECCA. Shut up Dean!

SAYID. My uncle used to work in an abattoir. Now he only eats Quorn.

BEX. I know what I'm gonna do Miss: I'm gonna marry a billionaire.

MISS HEDGE. Yes, well how about something a little bit more...realistic?

(Pause.)

BEX. A millionaire?

MISS HEDGE. And what do you want to be Sayid?

SAYID. Dunno Miss.

MISS HEDGE. What about you Cy?

CY. Dunno Miss.

MISS HEDGE. Fatimah?

FATIMAH. Dunno Miss.

MISS HEDGE. Levi?

LEVI. Dunno Miss.

MISS HEDGE. Mickey?

MICKEY. Dunno Miss.

MISS HEDGE. Vicki?

VICKI. Dunno Miss.

MISS HEDGE. Jamie?

(Beat.)

Jamie?

(Beat.)

Jamie New?!

*(And there's our hero, our **JAMIE**, Jamie New, lost in his own little world, performing a hand-vogue for the audience in his mind. He realises – looks 'round.)*

JAMIE. Oh? Me? Sorry Miss. Away with the fairies.

*(The **KIDS** snigger at this.)*

Yeah yeah, gay kid, ha ha –

MISS HEDGE. I said what do you want to do love? Careerwise?

JAMIE. Well, I dunno Miss. The future's just alive with enticing opportunities.

MISS HEDGE. Well I've got the results of your psychometric careers tests here, and Jamie love – you got Fork Lift Truck Driver.

JAMIE. Thanks miss. Dream come true.

[MUSIC NO. 01 'AND YOU DON'T EVEN KNOW IT']

'Cept the truth is, what I really wanna be – is a drag queen.

In this face.

In these lips.

In these hands.

In these legs.

In *her* shoes –

MISS HEDGE. What was that Jamie?

JAMIE. I said nice shoes Miss.

MISS HEDGE. Oh, thank you. They're Jimmy Choos.

Alright, sit down, shut up, eyes front – and the results of your Career Aptitude, Ability and Suitability Psychometric Evaluations are...

> (**MISS HEDGE** *starts handing out the test results.*)

JAMIE.

THERE'S A CLOCK ON THE WALL AND IT'S MOVING TOO SLOW

IT'S GOT HOURS TO KILL AND A LIFETIME TO GO

AND I'M HOLDING MY BREATH TILL I HEAR THE LAST BELL

THEN I'M COMING OUT HARD AND I'M GIVING 'EM HELL!

I'M A SUPERSTAR, AND YOU DON'T EVEN KNOW IT

IN A WONDER BRA, AND YOU DON'T EVEN KNOW IT

YOU'RE SO BLAH BLAH, AND YOU DON'T EVEN KNOW IT

I'M LIKE, AU REVOIR, AND YOU DON'T EVEN KNOW IT

THERE'S A PATH I'VE PLANNED

KIDS.

AND YOU DON'T EVEN KNOW IT

JAMIE.

TO THE PROMISED LAND

KIDS.

AND YOU DON'T EVEN KNOW IT

JAMIE.

YOU WON'T UNDERSTAND

KIDS.

AND YOU DON'T EVEN KNOW IT

JAMIE.

COS YOU'RE MY BACKING BAND

KIDS.

AND YOU DON'T EVEN KNOW IT

JAMIE.

AND IT'S THE JAMIE SHOW

KIDS.

AND YOU DON'T EVEN KNOW IT

JAMIE.

COS YOU'RE MEH, SO SO

KIDS.

AND YOU DON'T EVEN KNOW IT

JAMIE.

AND KINDA SLOW

KIDS.

AND YOU DON'T EVEN KNOW IT

JAMIE.

AND I'M GO GO GO

KIDS.

AND YOU DON'T EVEN KNOW IT!

JAMIE.

I GOT THE DREAMS, I GOT THE STYLE,
I GOT THE MOVES TO MAKE YOU SMILE!
SO KISS MY ASS GOODBYE!

JAMIE.	KIDS.
I'M GONNA BE THE ONE	COS I'M GONNA BE THE ONE

JAMIE.

I'M ON MY WAY, I WON'T BE TURNED
YOUR STUPID LESSONS I'VE UNLEARNED
AND I'LL BE FREE TO FLY

JAMIE.	KIDS.
I'M GONNA KISS THE SUN!	AND I'M GONNA KISS THE SUN!

JAMIE.

COS BABY I'M A HIT

KIDS.

AND YOU DON'T EVEN KNOW IT

JAMIE.

I'M IT

KIDS.

AND YOU DON'T EVEN KNOW IT

JAMIE.

YEAH, I'M LIT

KIDS.

AND YOU DON'T EVEN KNOW IT

JAMIE.

I'M A BLOCKBUSTER

KIDS.

AND YOU DON'T EVEN KNOW IT

JAMIE.

AND I'M RISING FAST!

KIDS.

AND YOU DON'T EVEN KNOW IT

JAMIE.

I'M AN ATOM BLAST

KIDS.

AND YOU DON'T EVEN KNOW IT

JAMIE.

AND THE PAST IS PAST

KIDS.

AND YOU DON'T EVEN KNOW IT

JAMIE.

I'LL BE FREE AT LAST!

KIDS.

AND YOU'RE ALL GONNA KNOW IT!

JAMIE.

YEAH THE WASTED YEARS, THE ENDLESS DAYS,
YOUR BORING NIGHTS, YOUR DULL CLICHÉS
GET OFF AND HIT THE TRACK

JAMIE.	**KIDS.**
I'M GONNA BE THE ONE	COS I'M GONNA BE THE ONE

JAMIE.

YOU'RE IN MY LANE, YOU'RE IN MY LIGHT,
GET OUT MY WAY, I'M TAKING FLIGHT
AND I AIN'T COMING BACK

JAMIE.	**KIDS.**
I'M GONNA KISS THE SUN!	AND I'M GONNA KISS THE SUN!

JAMIE.

AND IF EVER YOU FIND LIFE IS GETTING YOU DOWN
THERE'S A PARTY TO START IN A NEW PART OF TOWN

JAMIE.	**KIDS.**
WHERE THERE'S A GUEST LIST OF ONE AND THE NAME'S JAMIE NEW	OOH
AND IF YOU ASK ME REAL NICE I MIGHT SIGN YOU IN TOO	AH

JAMIE.

COS BABY I'M A HIT

KIDS.

AND YOU DON'T EVEN KNOW IT

JAMIE.

LEGIT

KIDS.

AND YOU DON'T EVEN KNOW IT

JAMIE.

BETTER GIVE ME ROOM

KIDS.

AND YOU DON'T EVEN KNOW IT

JAMIE.

FOR MY VA-VA-VOOM

KIDS.

AND YOU DON'T EVEN KNOW IT

JAMIE.

COS I'M COMING UP

KIDS.

AND YOU DON'T EVEN KNOW IT

JAMIE.

IN A DOUBLE-D CUP

KIDS.

AND YOU DON'T EVEN KNOW IT

JAMIE.

WHEN A BOY'S THIS STACKED

KIDS.

AND YOU DON'T EVEN KNOW IT

JAMIE.

HE'S THE HEADLINE ACT!

KIDS.

AND YOU DON'T EVEN KNOW IT!

JAMIE.

AND THE BOYS IN THE CLASS GO

BOYS.

OH-OH

JAMIE.

AND THE GIRLS IN THE CLASS GO

GIRLS.

HEY-OH

JAMIE.

ALL THE BOYS MAKE SOME NOISE, SAY

BOYS.

OH-OH

JAMIE.

EV'RY GIRL GIVE A TWIRL, SAY

GIRLS.

HEY-HEY-HEY!

JAMIE.

INTRODUCING MISS HEDGE! AND TEACHER SAYS:

MISS HEDGE.

KIDS KEEP BRAGGIN' AND MY DAYS KEEP DRAGGIN' BUT

MISS HEDGE & KIDS.

HEY HOO, WHATCHU GONNA DO

MISS HEDGE.

NO USE PREACHIN' COS I GAVE UP TEACHIN' BUT

MISS HEDGE & KIDS.

HEY HOO, WHATCHU GONNA DO?

MISS HEDGE.

I AIN'T LYIN' WHEN I CALL **KIDS.**	
THEM TROUBLE	TROUBLE
THEY BE CRAY CRAY	
DOUBLE ON DOUBLE	DOUBLE
YEAH YEAH NOWHERE	
BUSTIN' THEIR BUBBLE	BUBBLE
BRINGIN' IT DOWN ON	
THEIR HEADS LIKE	
RUBBLE	RUBBLE

MISS HEDGE.

TELL IT LIKE IT IS BUT THEY DON'T WANNA KNOW IT

LIFE DON'T OWE YOU, NO, YOU OWE IT

KIDS GROUP 1 (BEX, VICKI, LEVI, DEAN & MICKEY).

LIFE DON'T OWE YOU NO YOU OWE IT

LIFE DON'T OWE YOU NO YOU OWE IT

KIDS GROUP 1 (BEX, VICKI, LEVI, DEAN & MICKEY).	**KIDS GROUP 2 (BECCA, FATIMAH, SAYID & PRITTI).**
LIFE DON'T OWE YOU,	GO JAMIE!
NO, YOU OWE IT	GO JAMIE!

LIFE DON'T OWE YOU,
NO, YOU OWE IT
LIFE DON'T OWE YOU,
NO, YOU OWE IT
LIFE DON'T OWE YOU,
NO, YOU OWE -
GO!!!

IT'S YOUR BIRTHDAY!
IT'S YOUR BIRTHDAY!
GO JAMIE!
GO JAMIE!
GO JAMIE!
GO JAMIE!
GO!!!

JAMIE.

I GOT THE DREAMS, I GOT THE STYLE,
I GOT THE MOVES TO MAKE YOU SMILE!
SO KISS MY ASS GOODBYE

JAMIE.   **KIDS.**

I'M GONNA BE THE ONE   COS I'M GONNA BE THE ONE

JAMIE.

AND WHEN YOU'RE OLD, LIKE THIRTY-TWO,
YOU'LL ALL REMEMBER JAMIE NEW
THE KID WHO LEARNED TO FLY

JAMIE & KIDS.

AND I'M GONNA KISS THE SUN!

JAMIE.

COS BABY I'M A HIT

KIDS.

WE DON'T EVEN KNOW IT

JAMIE.

SO ADMIT

KIDS.

WE DON'T EVEN KNOW IT

JAMIE.

YEAH I'M A HIT

KIDS.

SHE DON'T EVEN KNOW IT

JAMIE.

JUST A BIT

KIDS.

HE DON'T EVEN KNOW IT

JAMIE.
> AND I'M SMOKING HOT

KIDS.
> WE DON'T EVEN KNOW IT

JAMIE.
> AND I GOT THE LOT

KIDS.
> WE DON'T EVEN KNOW IT

JAMIE.
> AND WHAT I GOT

KIDS.
> SHE DON'T EVEN KNOW IT

JAMIE.	**KIDS.**
YOU HAVE NOT, YEAH	OH
	WE DON'T EVEN KNOW IT!
YOU DON'T EVEN KNOW IT!	WE DON'T EVEN KNOW IT!
YOU DON'T EVEN KNOW IT!	SHE DON'T EVEN KNOW IT!
SHE DON'T EVEN KNOW IT!	HE DON'T EVEN KNOW IT!
HE DON'T EVEN KNOW IT!	WE DON'T EVEN KNOW IT!
YOU DON'T EVEN KNOW IT!	SHE DON'T EVEN KNOW IT!
YOU DON'T EVEN KNOW IT!	HE DON'T EVEN KNOW IT!

JAMIE & KIDS.
> AND YOU DON'T EVEN KNOW IT!

MISS HEDGE. What was that Jamie?

> (**JAMIE** *immediately goes into his shell.*)

JAMIE. Nothing Miss, just daydreaming, sorry.

DEAN. He's still away with them fairies Miss. Kissing 'em over a toadstool.

> (**JAMIE** *looks away, shamed.*)

MISS HEDGE. Dean –

DEAN. Queer.

MISS HEDGE. I'll pretend I didn't hear that. And what about you Dean? What future are you thinking of?

DEAN. I'm gonna have the most amazing, most glamorous, most exciting job in the world Miss – I'm gonna be a careers teacher.

MISS HEDGE. Jamie, you never answered my question: what do you want to be?

JAMIE. A...

(Almost says 'drag queen'.)

...performer.

MISS HEDGE. Oh, another one! Well join the queue love, with all the footballers and all the movie stars and the Sheffield's Next Top Models –

FATIMAH. That's so me, Miss.

JAMIE. No, what I want's not like that, I want to be –

MISS HEDGE. – No, come on class – *let's be real.* I wish I could tell you that you were all gonna achieve your dreams. But I'd be lying to you if I did, and that would be wrong. That would be cruel. Do you think me being here today teaching you was my first choice?

(The bell goes.)

Remember please – revision timetables. Your exams start in three weeks, this is not a drill. Good luck everyone. And happy birthday Jamie.

JAMIE. Thanks Miss.

MISS HEDGE. Jamie, wait up, what's that on your hand? Is that nail varnish?

JAMIE. Oh, I must have left a bit on, I was just messing, with me mum –

MISS HEDGE. What have I just said about keeping it real?

JAMIE. Yes Miss. Sorry Miss.

[MUSIC NO. 01A 'AND YOU DON'T EVEN KNOW IT (TAG)']

THERE'S A CLOCK ON THE WALL AND IT'S MOVING TOO SLOW,
IT'S GOT HOURS TO KILL AND A LIFETIME TO GO...

2. Jamie's House: Backyard

(Jamie's house is on a large council estate, on a road of similar, small houses with front-yard walls of red brick.)

(In the backyard: **RAY** *[Rayia], early forties, Jamie's mum's best friend and Jamie's de facto aunt, is hanging up 'HAPPY 16th BIRTHDAY' decorations and balloons.* **MARGARET**, *Jamie's mum, watches through the kitchen door, making tea.)*

RAY. You do! Come on Margaret, you know Dave.

MARGARET. I don't. I don't know a Dave.

RAY. Dave from't Fighting Cock – he does the meat raffle at quiz night.

MARGARET. Dave, with the big hands and runny eye?

RAY. Creepy Dave? Why would I be seeing Creepy Dave?

MARGARET. I don't know, you're always seeing somebody. Oh, is he the tall fella? Got a hairy back?

RAY. Chewbacca Dave?! No! You know Dave! *Dave* Dave! Fighting Cock Dave! Meat Raffle Dave!

MARGARET. Hang on, hang on...does he smell of mince?

RAY. That's the one! It's not so bad once he warms up a bit.

(She gives a low chuckle as **MARGARET** *comes out with two mugs of tea.)*

MARGARET. If you say so, hot-stuff. Here, it's a different brand of tea, tell me if it tastes funny but it were 20p off.

RAY. *(Winces.)* Nah, it's lovely. So how was your single's night?

MARGARET. Oh, that – I couldn't make it. Jamie needed help with his revision.

RAY. God's sake Margaret, let his dad help him.

MARGARET. He's no good at that stuff.

RAY. Oh well, let's add that to the great long list of Other Things He's Not Good At – including 'Turning Up To His Son's Birthday' – what's his excuse this time?

MARGARET. I don't know, I haven't spoke to him, he might still come.

RAY. Margaret! Stop making excuses for him! Look, you're still young, and you're proper gorgeous – when are you going to move on?

MARGARET. One day! Soon! Anyway, stop going on at me! I'm sick of men!

RAY. Bloody men. I'd have n'owt to do with them if I could help it. Problem is I can't help it.

JAMIE. *(Offstage.)* Mum!

(JAMIE approaches the back gate.)

RAY. Shhh – shhh – he's coming!

MARGARET. We're in't yard.

(JAMIE enters the backyard.)

RAY & MARGARET. SURPRISE!

(JAMIE takes in the decoration. It's humble to say the least, but he's genuinely thrilled.)

JAMIE. OMG! Is this all for me! Look at it, it's all glittery plastic, oh my God I love it!

(MARGARET gives him a big kiss.)

MARGARET. Happy birthday love.

JAMIE. Thanks Mum. Hiya Ray.

RAY. And another kiss from me, petal.

(She gives him a massive hug – they're incredibly close.)

MARGARET. So how was school?

JAMIE. Mortifying. I'm gonna be a forklift truck driver. Where's Dad?

MARGARET. *(Lying.)* He's gonna try and make it. You know what he's like, he's that lah-de-dah since he got a hatchback –

(RAY shoots MARGARET an angry look which MARGARET ignores.)

MARGARET. But he's not forgotten you, love – he sent you a card, see, arrived this morning.

JAMIE. Ace. Thank you.

(He rips open an envelope, revealing a fabulously inappropriate birthday card with a big, masculine vroom-vrooming racing car on the front.)

'Have A Full Throttle Birthday – Love Dad.' And a picture of a racing car. He knows me so well.

RAY. Penelope Pitstop drove a racing car.

JAMIE. Penelope Whatstop?

MARGARET. You're right! She did! Number Five in't Compact Pussycat.

JAMIE. Yeah, I bet Dad was thinking exactly that when he picked it. Ooh, twenty quid though, thanks Dad, you're a star.

MARGARET. Why've you got to be a forklift truck driver love?

JAMIE. It's destiny, according to Miss Hedge. You fill out this questionnaire and this computer somewhere reads your future. I got forklift truck driver or prison guard.

RAY. So this computer's definitely not met you then.

JAMIE. Pritti wants to be a doctor. She got veterinary assistant or stenographer.

MARGARET. Well, vets is medicine, in't it? She's nearly there.

JAMIE. Animals aren't people.

MARGARET. What about monkeys?

JAMIE. She don't wanna be a monkey doctor Mum.

(Beat.)

Miss Hedge asked me what I wanted to be. I could've said it then, I could've told them all. Instead I'm doomed to become a forklift truck driver. See – my future's here in black and white.

> *(He hands* **RAY** *his job evaluation form.* **RAY** *scans it.)*

RAY. Tha's right. It does say that.

JAMIE. I know!

RAY. And you know what I say?

> *(She pointedly rips the paper in half. Then rips it into shreds.)*

JAMIE. Mum! Ray! My forklifting dreams – she's ripping 'em up – she's chucking 'em away!

> *(***RAY*** *laughs and chucks the shreds up like confetti.)*

RAY. Ta-dah! And chuff off!

JAMIE. I love you Ray – you're so camp!

MARGARET. Anyway love, you couldn't drive a forklift even if you wanted to – not wearing these. Happy birthday.

> *(She hands* **JAMIE** *the box.)*

JAMIE. A shoebox?

RAY. Yeah. Take a guess what's in it.

> *(***JAMIE*** *opens the box – and gasps with delight!)*

JAMIE. Oh God – you didn't!

> *(And he removes from the box – a fantastic pair of red high heels in his size!)*

Wow. On. Chips. These are the ones, from Meadow Hall.

MARGARET. The ones you wanted.

JAMIE. But they're hundred and twenty quid! Hundred and twenty! Where'd you get money like that?!

MARGARET. I got it. Don't you worry.

RAY. Let's just say she went without.

> *(***JAMIE*** *stares at his mum, just humbled by what she's done.)*

JAMIE. Oh my first ever heels, thank you thank you thank you...

MARGARET. Woman in't shop said to me – 'Your daughter's got big feet.' I said to her – 'They're not for my daughter – they're for my son.' You should have seen the look on her face...

> (**JAMIE** *kicks his school shoes off, and then – still dressed in full school uniform – slips his new heels on for the very first time. He starts pacing in them – feeling his way.*)

JAMIE. Well they look amazing!

> (*He stumbles –* **MARGARET** *catches him – and he rights himself.*)

It's alright! She's down but she's not out!

RAY. Ay, chihuahua!!!!

JAMIE. Remember the first time I ever tried your shoes on Mum?

MARGARET. You fell downstairs in them, nearly broke your nose. I told your dad you got hit in't face with a rugby ball.

> (*Beat.*)

He was so proud...

JAMIE. Did you know he caught me once?

MARGARET. Did he?!

JAMIE. When I were eight. I was dancing 'round my bedroom in your sierra gold maxi-dress.

MARGARET. That old thing! So what did he say?

> (**JAMIE** *stops suddenly by the gate in the wall, remembering.*)

JAMIE. ...No, I can't do it Mum, I can't go out like this. What? Being seen – like this – by people!

RAY. Well if you want to be a drag queen you're gonna have to get used to being seen by people.

JAMIE. No. Miss Hedge is right...stupid dreams... I should just go be that forklifting prison guard. At least that's real.

MARGARET. Hey, I think you look absolutely fantastic. And you've got your dad to thank for them legs you know, you didn't get them off me. Why not take a little walk down't street if you like love, nobody's looking.

RAY. Here – we haven't lit the cake! Chuffing heck, you didn't hear me say that! Stay out here with your eyes shut!

(**RAY** and **MARGARET** scuttle back into the kitchen.)

[MUSIC NO. 02 'THE WALL IN MY HEAD']

JAMIE.

IT WAS SOMETHING HE SAID,
SOMETHING HE SAID.
HIS WORDS BUILT A WALL
A WALL INSIDE MY HEAD.
JUST ONE LITTLE THING
DIDN'T MEAN THAT MUCH TO HIM,
BUT IT KEEPS BUILDING, AND BUILDING, AND BUILDING
THIS WALL IN MY HEAD.
THIS WALL IN MY HEAD.

JUST ONE TINY THOUGHT
IT STARTED OUT SO SMALL
THE THOUGHT MADE A BRICK,
THE BRICKS MADE A WALL
AND THE WALL KEEPS ME DOWN
AND THE WALL TRIPS ME UP
AND IT KEEPS BUILDING, AND BUILDING, AND BUILDING
THIS WALL IN MY HEAD.
THIS WALL IN MY HEAD.

AND HERE I STAND WITH ME FEET STUCK TO THE FLOOR
AS I SHOUT DOWN THE STREET, SCREAMING FOR MORE!

JAMIE.

> OVER THE WALL!
> OVER THE WALL
> I SEE MY FUTURE STANDING TALL!
> OVER THE WALL!
> OVER THE WALL
> I CAN BELIEVE I'D HAVE IT ALL!
> SO I KEEP CLIMBING, AND CLIMBING, AND CLIMBING
> THIS WALL IN MY HEAD, HEAD, HEAD.
> I'LL KEEP ON CLIMBING, AND CLIMBING, AND CLIMBING
> THIS WALL IN MY HEAD, HEAD, HEAD.
>
> THIS WALL IN MY HEAD
> THIS WALL IN MY HEAD...
>
> IT WAS SOMETHING HE SAID,
> JUST ONE LITTLE THING
> THE THOUGHT LEFT A SCAR
> THE WORDS LEFT A STING
> THOSE WORDS ARE THE WALLS
> THAT STILL HOLD ME IN
> AND THEY KEEP BUILDING, AND
> BUILDING, AND BUILDING, AND
> BUILDING AND –
>
> DON'T FALL – I'M FINDING ME FEET,
> THERE'S SHOES TO BE FILLED
> BUT THIS WALL – IS HARDER TO BEAT
> WHEN IT'S ONE YOU HELPED BUILD.
>
> OVER THE WALL!
> OVER THE WALL
> I SEE MY FUTURE STANDING TALL!
> OVER THE WALL!
> OVER THE WALL
> I CAN BELIEVE I'D HAVE IT ALL!

JAMIE.	**ENSEMBLE.** *(Offstage.)*
SO I KEEP CLIMBING,	CLIMBING,
AND CLIMBING, AND CLIMBING	CLIMBING, CLIMBING
THIS WALL IN MY HEAD,	HEAD,
HEAD, HEAD.	HEAD, HEAD.

I'LL KEEP ON CLIMBING,	CLIMBING,
AND CLIMBING, AND CLIMBING	CLIMBING, CLIMBING
THIS WALL IN MY HEAD,	HEAD,
HEAD, HEAD	HEAD, HEAD.
OH, I'LL KEEP CLIMBING,	CLIMBING,
AND CLIMBING,	CLIMBING,
AND CLIMBING, AND CLIMBING,	CLIMBING, CLIMBING,
AND CLIMBING, AND CLIMBING,	CLIMBING, CLIMBING,
AND CLIMBING, AND CLIMBING,	CLIMBING, CLIMBING,
AND HAND OVER HAND OVER	CLIMBING, CLIMBING,
HAND OVER BRICK OVER	CLIMBING, CLIMBING,
HAND OVER BRICK OVER	CLIMBING, CLIMBING,
HAND OVER BRICK OVER	CLIMBING, CLIMBING,
CLIMBIN',	CLIMBING, CLIMBING,
CLIMBIN',	CLIMBING, CLIMBING,
CLIMBIN',	CLIMBING, CLIMBING,
CLIMBING THIS WALL IN MY	CLIMBING, CLIMBING,
HEAD...	CLIMBING, CLIMBING,
THIS WALL IN MY HEAD...	CLIMBING, CLIMBING,
	CLIMBING, CLIMBING,
	CLIMBING, CLIMBING,
	HOOH

THIS WALL IN MY HEAD...

> (**MARGARET** *and* **RAY** *emerge with a cake blazing with candles.*)

RAY. Here! Here! Blow 'em out, quick!
   The wax is burning me thumbs to chuffery!

MARGARET. Make a wish son.

> (**JAMIE** *looks over the wall...makes his wish. Blows the candles out.*)

> (*Blackout.*)

[MUSIC NO. 02A 'SCENE CHANGE']

3. Mayfield School: Classroom

(The classroom is empty, quiet – except for **PRITTI**, *working alone through a pile of books, the writing on the whiteboard: 'YEAR 11 REVISION SESSION'.)*

*(**BEX** and **BECCA** enter.)*

BEX. Alright Pritti, didn't know you were coming to this.

PRITTI. Yes, oh, I mean, it's so important in't it?

BECCA. You're telling me.

BEX. It's all I can think about at the minute. Like the band –

BECCA. – the food –

BEX. – the flowers –

BECCA. – the dress –

BEX. – long sleeve –

BECCA. – short sleeve –

BEX. – backless –

BECCA. – strapless –

BEX. – crystals and sequins and ruffles –

BECCA. – or plain.

PRITTI. What are you talking about?

BECCA. The School Prom. This is School Prom Planning.

PRITTI. No. That's next door. This is a group revision session.

BEX. So where's the group?

PRITTI. Well... I'm it.

BECCA. Revision session? Bloody hell Bex we are *well* in't wrong place.

*(**JAMIE** enters as **BEX** and **BECCA** are leaving.)*

JAMIE. Alright girls.

BEX. Wrong room Jamie – prom planning's next door.

JAMIE. No, I'm here to revise.

BECCA. Why?

JAMIE. Cos I promised Pritti.

BEX. Wow. Funzilla alert.

JAMIE. What dress are you wearing though?

BECCA & BEX. *It's a surprise.*

JAMIE. Bet it's lush though, oh you lucky things.

BECCA & BEX. *Laters!*

> (**BEX** *and* **BECCA** *exit, joining the prom planning session in the classroom next door.*)

JAMIE. Laters...please don't leave me...

> *(Beat.)*

Ugh – *revision!* It's so boring.

PRITTI. Go on, go. I know you'd rather be next door with them, prom planning.

JAMIE. Shut up! I promised didn't I? I want good grades too. Besides, you're my best friend.

PRITTI. *(Grinning.)* Am I?

JAMIE. Course you are, shut up you daft idiot.

PRITTI. Am I your...

> *(Trying to remember the word.)*

...*fag hag?*

> (**JAMIE** *bursts out laughing.*)

JAMIE. Wash your mouth out Pritti Pasha – where have you been learning words like that?

PRITTI. I watched a documentary, about Canal Street. My dad came in and I had to pretend I was just really interested in waterways.

JAMIE. Well you can be my fag hag if you want. Here – start by helping your stupid GBF revise so he can pass some of his exams for once.

PRITTI. You're not stupid Jamie. Your brain's just the wrong shape for school.

JAMIE. I like that!

> *(Whispers.)* Listen, if you promise not to tell anyone, I've got something to show you!

PRITTI. Is it gross? I don't want to see it if it's got willies.

> (**JAMIE** *opens his schoolbag and takes out the shoes.*)

Oh my days – they're so glamorous! Who are they for?

> (*Pause.*)

JAMIE. Me.

PRITTI. You? What do you mean 'you'? How do you mean you? Do you mean...to wear?

JAMIE. Yes.

> (*Pause.*)

PRITTI. On your feet?

JAMIE. No Pritti, I'm gonna pierce me nipples and swing 'em off me tits – yes, yes on me feet!

PRITTI. Jamie...are you saying...

> (*Beat.*)

What are you saying?

JAMIE. You remember when we were little, and we used to play dress-up – and I'd always be Carol Vorderman – well, for me...that's a game that I don't want to stop playing.

PRITTI. Dressing up as a woman?

JAMIE. Yeah.

PRITTI. Do you want to *be* a woman?

JAMIE. No. I want to be a boy. Who sometimes wants to be a girl.

PRITTI. Is it...sexual?

JAMIE. No! It's fun. It's *wonderful.* I want to be a drag queen. For a job. You can do that you know, make some money. Just not on't Parson Cross, can you imagine! Well...what do you think?

> (**PRITTI** *stares at him long and hard, working out what to say.*)

PRITTI. ...I don't understand why *girls* want to wear all that stuff – the makeup and the hair and them ridiculous shoes, I mean no offense but...so for a *boy* to want it –

JAMIE. Oh my God – you think I'm weird don't you? You think I'm a freak!

PRITTI. No – it's not...not a *freak*... I just...

(*Beat.*)

I do think it's weird. Yes. But I guess that's the point in't it – everyone thinks I'm weird too. I'm a Muslim girl with a Hindu first name – I mean thanks Mum! You should see some of the looks they gimme at mosque.

JAMIE. Yes Pritti. Me, being a drag queen, in Sheffield, is exactly like that.

PRITTI. I'm just saying – that's us, weirdos together. I don't fit in because I want to be a doctor. You don't fit in because you want to dress up.

JAMIE. (*Points to* PRITTI.) High achiever.
(*Points to self.*) High heels.

(PRITTI *laughs.*)

PRITTI. Exactly – us highs have to stick together through them lows.

JAMIE. So we're still mates?

PRITTI. Bezzy mates, hashtag foreva.

JAMIE. Oh thank God – I mean Allah, or whatever – hey you're the first person I've told, apart from Mum and Ray – look I'm shaking.

PRITTI. So when are you gonna wear them?

JAMIE. Just...at home, walking about.

PRITTI. Not in public?

JAMIE. Are you kidding me? This is Sheffield, not San Francisco!

PRITTI. (*Jokingly.*) You could wear them to that stupid prom.

JAMIE. Yeah, I don't think they'll go with my tux.

(**DEAN** *passes the door, decides to be annoying.*)

DEAN. Alright Jamie. Well well well – if it in't Tweedle-Dum and Tweedle-Bummer.

(**JAMIE** *hides the shoes under his desk.*)

JAMIE. Go away Dean, you're not funny.

DEAN. I am, I'm hilarious, me. What's gay and says 'ow'?

JAMIE. I don't know.

(**DEAN** *clips* **JAMIE** *'round the side of the head.*)

Ow! Oh get lost Dean – I don't have time for this, I can't be bothered.

DEAN. Oh, bless, can't you? And what about you, you fat sweaty swotty spotty speccy virgin?

JAMIE. Don't you *dare* call her that!

DEAN. What? She is. Just like you're a gay gay gay gay gay gay gay gay gay –

(*Thinks.*)

gay boy.

(*And for the first time in his life –* **JAMIE** *answers back:*)

JAMIE. Yeah Dean, I'm gay. I *am* gay – so if *I* call me gay then being called gay in't an insult, is it? Cos I am bent, and I am queer, and I'm a great big sissy boy – you tragic meat head bad breath povvo waste of space nobody.

DEAN. I don't have bad breath!

JAMIE. That's not what Becca says.

DEAN. Get stuffed Jamie New.

(*He scowls and stalks away.*)

PRITTI. Oh my days look at you! You've always been out – but now you're like *out* out – you're totally fearless! You're Emmeline Pankhurst!

JAMIE. Thanks. Who's she?

(**PRITTI** *thinks how to explain this in Jamie-speak.*)

PRITTI. She were like Beyoncé back in't day.

JAMIE. No! Do you think! Shut up!

(**PRITTI** *takes Jamie's shoes out and plonks them on the desk.*)

PRITTI. Put these on.

JAMIE. What!

PRITTI. Put. These. On.

JAMIE. I can't! Not in public!

PRITTI. What you just showed me then, what you said to Dean, that *fire* in you – you find it again and put these on.

JAMIE. I can't! You're mad! Pritti Pasha you're delusional!

PRITTI. You can. You really can. You just put them on.

JAMIE. Oh yeah – like it's that easy.

PRITTI. It is. You just stick a toe in. Simple as. Even that Kim Kardashian can do it. I mean, that's literally all she does. Jamie, stop waiting for permission to be you. Wear these to prom.

JAMIE. With my tux?

PRITTI. No. With a dress.

[MUSIC NO. 03 'SPOTLIGHT']

COS THE PARTY'S JUST STARTING
AND YOU DON'T WANT TO MISS IT
THE PARTY'S JUST STARTING
ALMOST SO CLOSE YOU CAN KISS IT

DON'T WAIT FOR TOMORROW
BE HAPPY TODAY
AND ALL OF THOSE STUPID PEOPLE –
WHO CARES WHAT THEY SAY?

I KNOW IT'S NOT EASY
BUT I KNOW YOU'RE STRONG
AND I KNOW THAT SOMEWHERE
THEY'RE PLAYING YOUR SONG

PRITTI.

OUT OF THE DARKNESS
INTO THE SPOTLIGHT
EV'RYONE'S WAITING, JAMIE
IN A PLACE WHERE YOU BELONG
SOMEWHERE'S A PARTY
THAT CAN'T START WITHOUT YOU
SOMEWHERE THE DJ
IS PLAYING YOUR SONG

(From the prom-planning classroom next door comes the sound of the **GIRLS** *singing.)*

GIRLS (BECCA, BEX, VICKI & FATIMAH).

WHEN THE CURTAIN'S GOING UP
ALL EYES ON ME!
WHEN THE LIGHTS ARE GOING DOWN
ALL EYES ON ME!
WHEN THE CROWDS ARE SHOWING UP
ALL EYES ON ME!
COS TONIGHT'S A-GOING DOWN
ALL EYES ON ME!

PRITTI.	**GIRLS.**
HEY, CAN YOU HEAR THEM?	WHEN THE CURTAIN'S GOING UP
	ALL EYES ON ME!
THAT'S YOUR AUDIENCE WAITING	WHEN THE LIGHTS ARE GOING DOWN
	ALL EYES ON ME!
THERE'LL BE QUEUES 'ROUND THE THEATRE	WHEN THE CROWDS ARE SHOWING UP
	ALL EYES ON ME!
FOR ALL THE SHOWS YOU'RE CREATING	COS TONIGHT'S A-GOING DOWN
	ALL EYES ON ME!
AND MAYBE THERE'LL BE CURTAINS	COS YOU ONLY GET ONE SHOT!
	ALL EYES ON ME!

HUNG IN VELVET
   MAROON

AND MAYBE THERE'LL BE
   ICE CREAM,
IN A TINY TUB,

PRITTI & ENSEMBLE.

WITH A BUILT-IN SPOON!

PRITTI.

OUT OF THE DARKNESS,
INTO THE SPOTLIGHT

GIRLS.

ALL EYES ON ME

PRITTI.

EV'RYONE'S WAITING,
   JAMIE
COS THAT'S WHERE YOU
   BELONG
AND SOMEWHERE'S A
   PARTY

GIRLS.

ALL EYES ON ME

PRITTI.

THAT CAN'T START
   WITHOUT YOU

GIRLS.

ALL EYES ON ME

PRITTI.

AND SOMEWHERE THE DJ
IS PLAYING YOUR SONG

GIRLS.

WHEN THE CURTAIN'S GOING UP
WHEN THE LIGHTS ARE GOING DOWN

PRITTI.

PLAYING YOUR SONG

SO WE GOTTA TAKE THIS
   CHANCE!
ALL EYES ON ME!
WHEN A SISTER LOOKS
   THIS HOT
ALL EYES ON ME!

ENSEMBLE.

AH

ENSEMBLE.

AH

GIRLS.

> WHEN THE CROWDS ARE SHOWING UP
> COS TONIGHT'S A-GOIN' DOWN

PRITTI.

> COS THE PARTY'S JUST STARTING...

> *(She pushes the shoes towards* **JAMIE** *– then gingerly, he slips a foot into each shoe. And there he is. In public. In heels.)*

You did it!

JAMIE. I did! And I am wearing these to prom!

[MUSIC CUE NO. 03A 'SPOTLIGHT REPRISE (STAR OF THE SHOW)']

Cos sometimes Pritti Pasha, you've gotta grab life by the balls! Then you take those balls, you tuck them between your legs and you put your best chuffing frock on!

> OUT OF THE DARKNESS!
> INTO THE SPOTLIGHT!
> A TEENAGE SENSATION IS COMING

PRITTI.

> THE NEW STAR OF THE SHOW!

JAMIE.

> GIVE ME THE ENCORE!

JAMIE & PRITTI.

> THE STANDING OVATION!

JAMIE.	**PRITTI & CHORUS.**
WATCH ME GO!	AH

JAMIE. Jamie New: The Boy So Nice He Came Out Twice!

4. Victor's Secret

(Victor's Secret is a dress shop for drag queens. Everything is OTT and bold or day-glow colours, sequins, feathers and lace abound, and several mannequins are decked out in splendid fabulousness. There are various, slightly faded posters taking up the walls depicting the same drag queen in numerous costumes and poses.)

(HUGO, a dour man who looks quite out of place here, sits by the till reading the paper.)

(The door pings open – and JAMIE pokes his head inside. HUGO doesn't look up.)

HUGO. Well come in if you're coming in, don't just linger like an old nun's fart.

(JAMIE gulps – and enters.)

Welcome to Victor's Secret. Drag Couturiers to the stars!

(He gestures theatrically, then buries himself in the paper again, writing JAMIE off for being too young.)

JAMIE. Um...are you Victor?

HUGO. No love, I'm Hugo. *Victor's Secret* is a play on words, like Victoria's Secret, except Victor's Secret is the one he doesn't tell his wife. Originally I was going to call it 'The Tuck Shop'. Think about it.

(Beat.)

And what's your name?

JAMIE. Jamie. Can I...can I try one of these on?

HUGO. Knock yourself out lad. You tears it, you wears it.

(JAMIE picks up a dress – running his fingers across the fabric like it's spun gold, hypnotised.)

HUGO. So, what's it for then? Fancy Dress party? Let me guess – *Rocky Horror*.

JAMIE. No. It's for me. To wear. It's not a costume.

> *(Deep breath, oh God, here goes…)*

I want to be a drag queen.

> *(Pause. And now **HUGO**'s interested.)*

HUGO. How old are you Jamie?

JAMIE. Sixteen. Just.

HUGO. Sixteen. They're getting younger and younger. Whilst I just curl up here in an ossifying ball growing ever more fabulous. So anything grab your fancy?

JAMIE. How about all of them? I don't know where to start.

HUGO. You have to let the dress choose you.

JAMIE. Okay, right, okay…

> *(He moves between the dresses – before selecting a blood-red number: sequins and diamanté.)*

…this one!

> *(**HUGO** gasps!!!)*

HUGO. Oh Jamie, steady yourself, calm down, easy lad, easy. The dress you now hold in your hands was once worn by *her*.

JAMIE. Her? Her who?

HUGO. *Loco Chanelle* herself!

JAMIE. Who's Loco Chanelle?

HUGO. Who's Loco Chanelle! WHO'S LOCO CHANELLE! SHE'S LOCO CHANELLE!!!

> *(He gestures to the various posters.)*

The greatest drag queen what ever lived – the defining icon of a golden age – a goddess made flesh, put upon this earth to elevate us humble mortals into new levels of ecstasy!

(He realises how camp he's got – dials it all down.)

I mean, she were alright. If you like that sort of thing.

So, we've found your dress – now, does she have a name?

JAMIE. What?

HUGO. Does your drag queen have a name?

JAMIE. Well I've thought, a bit, you know, brainstormed, but I don't really –

HUGO. Out with it – come on, you'll never know if you don't say. What is it?

> *(JAMIE sheepishly takes a piece of paper from his pocket, unfolds it, taking his time, deep breath, reads it:)*

JAMIE. Sandra Banana.

HUGO. *(Unimpressed.)* Sandra. Banana.

JAMIE. I know!

HUGO. Sandra Banana?!

JAMIE. I know!

HUGO. You'll have to do better than Sandra Banana! Your name's your brand! Take it seriously! I mean, who's ever heard of Archibald Leach?

JAMIE. Who's Archibald Leach?

HUGO. That's Cary Grant's real name.

JAMIE. Who's Cary Grant?

HUGO. Oh bloody hell! My point is – all *this* is a process of...*becoming.*

JAMIE. Becoming what?

HUGO. Becoming *more.* She's in there Jamie, she really is, just waiting to burst forth from you. Like that bloody great worm out John Hurt's chest in't first *Alien* movie.

JAMIE. I get it, I do, and she is in there...but for now – I was just going to go to prom in a dress.

HUGO. Prom? As in 'School Prom'?

JAMIE. Yeah. Why, do you think it's stupid?

HUGO. I think... I think...

> *(Long pause.)*

> CHUFFING HELLFIRE!!! You don't ask much of yourself, do you lad!

JAMIE. Is it mad? Is it too much?

> *(He puts the red dress back on the rail.)*

HUGO. Honestly Jamie... I'd be lying if I said I didn't have concerns. I mean people...they can be ballbags. And teenagers...they can be *big bouncing* ballbags. What if they turn on you? Have you thought of that?

JAMIE. So don't you think I should go?

HUGO. No Jamie – you *have* to go! In honour of all your fallen comrades what come before you! This is war my son, you're a warrior now, and a warrior needs the very best armour.

JAMIE. What's my armour?

HUGO. *Her.*

> *(He grabs the red dress from the rail – and hands it back to **JAMIE**!)*

> Drag Queens should be *warriors*. Performance is a *battle*. Makeup is *armour*. Drag is fierce, it's *angry*! You have to create a *persona* – you can't just be a boy in a dress. A boy in a dress is something to be laughed at – a Drag Queen is something to be *feared*.

JAMIE. But I don't want to make people scared of me.

HUGO. Shoot first, or they'll shoot you down. First rule of drag. Look at her – look at everything she is!

> *(He gestures to the posters of Loco Chanelle.)*

JAMIE. 'Loco Chanelle, The Killer Queen In The Blood Red Dress'. Wow. So what happened to her?

HUGO. She's standing right here.

JAMIE. Where?

HUGO. Here.

> *(And he strikes a pose! **JAMIE** looks from **HUGO** – to Loco!)*

JAMIE. No! No way! I mean – no! No way! No! But you're like a different person!

HUGO. THAT'S good armour.

JAMIE. How did you do it? How did you start...*creating* her?

HUGO. It's all about the backstory, the fiercer the better. Where she's come from, where she's going to, and how you met her on't way.

JAMIE. So Loco Chanelle, did she have like a backstory an' all?

HUGO. She did. A good one. I wish I could remember it all now.

JAMIE. Try – go on.

HUGO. To be honest Jamie pet, it's been such a long time since I put the old wig on, let me see, right, okay, yes, I think it sort of went something like –

[MUSIC NO. 04 'THE LEGEND OF LOCO CHANELLE (AND THE BLOOD RED DRESS)']

HUGO.	**TENORS & BASSES.** (*Offstage.*)
ONCE IN A LIFETIME!	AH
THERE WILL RISE A HERO!	
WHOSE APPROACHING FOOTSTEPS	AH
WILL CAUSE THE EARTH TO QUAKE!	
ONCE IN A LIFETIME!	AH
THEY'LL BAPTISE A HERO	
IN THE BLOOD SHE LEFT IN HER WAKE!	AH
THE LEGEND OF LOCO CHANELLE!	AH

(*He ushers* **JAMIE** *behind a screen to change into the dress. As* **HUGO** *sings,* **DRAG QUEENS** *enter to help enact his story:* **YOUNG LOCO CHANELLE**, *the villainous* **JOHN** *and* **THE OTHER WOMAN**.)

HUGO.

Right – strip!

I'LL SING A STORY NOW OF WAY OUT WEST
OF MADAM LOCO AND THE BLOOD RED DRESS
AND OF THE MAN WHO DIDN'T TREAT HER RIGHT

DRAG QUEENS.

YOU SEE THAT DRESS –
WELL, IT STARTED OUT WHITE.

> (**YOUNG LOCO CHANELLE** *removes her coat,*
> *revealing a sparkling white dress, identical*
> *in all but colour to Jamie's dress.*)

HUGO.

SHE WAS THE SWEETEST THING YOU EVER SEEN
RAISED ON A CATTLE RANCH IN SOUTHEY GREEN
SHE WAS A BEAUTY QUEEN IN '79
AND SPENT HER SUMMER ON THE GREYHOUND LINE

DRAG QUEENS.

LOCO

HUGO.

SHE KNEW THAT EV'RY QUEEN MUST HAVE HER CROWN

DRAG QUEENS.

LOCO

HUGO.

SO SHE SET OFF TO A PLACE CALLED
'LONDON TOWN'

DRAG QUEENS.

LOCO

HUGO.

WHERE STREETS ARE PAVED WITH GOLD AND LIT WITH
DREAMS

DRAG QUEENS.

LOCO

HUGO.

AND MAGPIES COME TO GATHER ALL THAT GLEAMS

DRAG QUEENS.

LOCO

HUGO.

A SIMPLE GIRL, SHE'D NEVER TRAVELLED FAR

DRAG QUEENS.

LOCO

HUGO.

BUT IN HER HEART THERE BURNED A SUPERSTAR!

DRAG QUEENS.

LOCO

HUGO.

SHE HIT 'EM HARD AND SWORE SHE'D GIVE 'EM HELL!
THE LEGEND OF...

DRAG QUEENS.

LOCO CHANELLE!

JAMIE. I love it! You came up with all of this!

HUGO. Well I did go to London, and I was a simple girl. Other names and identifying details have been changed to protect the privacy of certain individuals.

SHE'D NOT A SINGLE FRIEND TO COUNT UPON

TENORS & BASSES. *(Offstage.)*

LOCO CHANELLE

HUGO.

UNTIL, IN CAMDEN, MET A MAN NAMED JOHN

TENORS & BASSES. *(Offstage.)*

LOCO CHANELLE

HUGO.

HE LIKED HER LIPSTICK, AND HE LOVED HER WIG
HE TOLD HER:

JOHN.

BABY DOLL, I'LL MAKE YOU BIG!

TENORS & BASSES. *(Offstage.)*

LOCO CHANELLE

JOHN.

STICK WITH ME KIDDO AND THIS CITY'S YOURS

TENORS & BASSES. *(Offstage.)*

LOCO CHANELLE

JOHN.

THE FAME, THE FORTUNE, THE PERPETUAL APPLAUSE

TENORS & BASSES. *(Offstage.)*

LOCO CHANELLE

HUGO.

SHE TRUSTED JOHNNY, SO SHE SPENT THE NIGHT
WHO KNEW A WOLF HAD SUCH A CHARMING BITE?

TENORS & BASSES. *(Offstage.)*

LOCO

HUGO.

BUT JOHNNY WAS AN AGENT, NOT A GENT

TENORS & BASSES. *(Offstage.)*

LOCO

HUGO.

AND TOOK MORE THAN THE USUAL TEN PERCENT

TENORS & BASSES. *(Offstage.)*

LOCO

HUGO.

AND THOUGH HE PROMISED MS CHANELLE THE EARTH

TENORS & BASSES. *(Offstage.)*

LOCO

HUGO.

SHE SOON DISCOVERED WHAT HIS WORD WAS WORTH

ALTOS & TENORS. *(Offstage.)*

LOCO

HUGO.

ON OP'NING NIGHT – THE AUDIENCE WAS PACKED

ALTOS & TENORS. *(Offstage.)*

LOCO

HUGO.

WHEN SHE CAUGHT HIM SCREWING WITH A YOUNGER
ACT

ALTOS & TENORS. *(Offstage.)*

LOCO

HUGO.

IN FLAGRANTE IN THE FINCHLEY NOVOTEL
THE TRAGEDY OF...

TENORS & BASSES. *(Offstage.)*
LOCO CHANELLE!

> *(***YOUNG LOCO CHANELLE*** catches **JOHN** in a clinch with **THE OTHER WOMAN**.)*

JAMIE. It's so melodramatic! I wish my life was like this!
HUGO. You stick with me kid – it will be!
THE SEATS WERE SOLD OUT TO THE LAST RESERVES
TENORS & BASSES. *(Offstage.)*
LOCO CHANELLE
HUGO.
SHE SAID:
YOUNG LOCO CHANELLE.
I NEED A DRINK TO CALM ME NERVES
TENORS & BASSES. *(Offstage.)*
LOCO CHANELLE
HUGO.
THEN SHE SAW JOHNNY, WITH HIS TIE ASKEW
HER LOOK WAS LOADED, AND HER GUN WAS, TOO
TENORS & BASSES. *(Offstage.)*
LOCO CHANELLE
YOUNG LOCO CHANELLE.
HERE'S TO YA JOHNNY, HAVE A SHOT TO START
TENORS & BASSES. *(Offstage.)*
LOCO CHANELLE
HUGO.
AND THEN SHE SMILED AND SHOT HIM THROUGH THE HEART
TENORS & BASSES. *(Offstage.)*
LOCO CHANELLE
HUGO.
HER DRESS WAS PUREST WHITE 'TIL JOHNNY BLED
AND TURNED HER VIRGIN GOWN TO

HUGO.
DEEPEST RED

ALTOS, TENORS & BASSES. *(Offstage.)*
HA

(**YOUNG LOCO CHANELLE** *crouches over* **JOHN***'s body and rubs the blood from his fatal wound across her white dress – turning it a fantastic, vivid red.*)

TENORS & BASSES. *(Offstage.)*

LOCO

HUGO.

SHE STRODE ONTO THE STAGE, A CRIMSON QUEEN,

TENORS & BASSES. *(Offstage.)*

LOCO

HUGO.

AND KILLED THE CROWD BY STEALING EV'RY SCENE

TENORS & BASSES. *(Offstage.)*

LOCO

HUGO.

AND SOON HER FANS WERE QUEUING 'ROUND THE BLOCK

TENORS & BASSES. *(Offstage.)*

LOCO

HUGO.

TO SEE THE DIVA IN THE BLOOD RED FROCK

ALTOS, TENORS & BASSES. *(Offstage.)*

LOCO

HUGO.

AND THAT, MY DEAR, IS HOW A STAR SHALL RISE

ALTOS, TENORS & BASSES. *(Offstage.)*

LOCO

HUGO.

WITH RUBY LIPS AND MURDER IN HER EYES!

ALTOS, TENORS & BASSES. *(Offstage.)*

LOCO

HUGO.

'TIL ONE DAY, TO AVOID A PRISON CELL

TENORS & BASSES. *(Offstage.)*

LOCO

HUGO.

MISS LOCO VANISHED LIKE A MAGIC SPELL

TENORS & BASSES. *(Offstage.)*

LOCO

HUGO.

AND WHERE SHE IS NOW – NO! I'LL NEVER TELL!

ALTOS, TENORS & BASSES.

HUGO.   *(Offstage.)*

THAT'S THE LEGEND OF   LOCO

ALL.

LOCO CHANELLE!

> *(The* **DRAG QUEENS** *vanish from the stage as* **JAMIE** *emerges from the cubicle, feeling vulnerable in his dress – so exposed.)*

JAMIE. I'm not sure if it, if I...what do you think? Is it fierce?

HUGO. Jamie – it's *amazing*. It's perfection. It's *you*.

JAMIE. Do you think?

HUGO. I *know*.

JAMIE. Thanks.

> *(Beat.)*

So did you really shoot a man on your opening night?

HUGO. No, but I was once sick in a friend's grave at a funeral.

JAMIE. No but Hugo, tell me – did you really run away? Did you really make it big? Is there really a Novotel in Finchley?

HUGO. Jamie! Never ask a legend to explain herself!

JAMIE. Well I don't know why you stopped! Was John real? Did he break your heart?

> *(Pause.)*

HUGO. You know what you need? Before your Prom? A dry run. A chance to road test the New You. Have you heard of Legs Eleven?

JAMIE. The drag night at Social? Who hasn't? Even the straight boys go there, all stag nights and office parties.

HUGO. Well, I used to perform at Legs Eleven and I'm a good friend of them girls. If you like I could put in a word for you? Get you on as the opening act?

JAMIE. Oh my God! Yes – amazing!

HUGO. I mean, it's only Sheffield, but if you can survive on that stage, them kids at that prom won't be able to touch you. You'll be bulletproof for life.

JAMIE. So my 'act' – how does it work?

HUGO. Well, you get out there and you slay them! And if you have any doubts, you just ask yourself: 'What Would Loco Chanelle do?'

JAMIE. ...She'd shoot from the hip.

HUGO. You got it kid! Now that'll be ninety pounds for the dress. I'd prefer cash but diamonds are acceptable.

JAMIE. Ninety...oh.

HUGO. Oh forget the money!

JAMIE. You're giving it to me?

HUGO. Oh poppet – no one's that rich anymore – but I can loan it to you for your show at Legs Eleven, just for the night. How does that sound? Take these too – on the house, to be getting on with. Think of them as your practice hot pants.

> *(He hands **JAMIE** a pair of black sequin hot pants.)*

Bless – I feel like I should weld training wheels on them.

JAMIE. I can't thank you enough Hugo.

HUGO. It's a long climb to go petal – and you haven't won yet. Save your thanks for when you're safely out t'other side.

JAMIE. See ya Hugo. And thanks.

> *(He shakes **HUGO**'s hand, respectful. **HUGO**, touched, replies with a little curtsey.)*

HUGO. See you soon Jamie. Take care. Take care.

> *(**JAMIE** leaves.)*

[MUSIC NO. 04A 'LOCO CHANELLE (REPRISE)']

BUT THERE'S ONE FINAL TWIST I DIDN'T TELL
ABOUT THE FATE BEFALLING MS CHANELLE
HER STAR BURNED BRIGHT AND FAR TOO HOT TO TOUCH
BUT BURN AND YOU CAN BURN YOURSELF TOO MUCH
SHE FLEW TOO NEAR THE SUN AND SO SHE FRIED
HER GREATEST FOE – HER FOOLISH BOASTFUL PRIDE
SHE CLIMBED SO HIGH – THEN DOWN SO FAR SHE FELL
THAT WAS THE END OF LOCO CHANELLE

5. Street Corner Bench

(**MARGARET** *sitting on an ordinary bench a few streets away from home, on edge. She checks her watch for the thousandth time, pulls out her phone and dials. It rings, then goes to voicemail. She hangs up, so frustrated. Before she can call again, a nondescript man,* **JAMIE'S DAD**, *strolls casually towards her.*)

MARGARET. Oh here he is! What time do you call this?! I've been ringing and ringing,

(**JAMIE'S DAD** *takes his phone out, glances at it.*)

JAMIE'S DAD. Look at that, must have switched it off, sorry.

MARGARET. I wish I could switch *you* off!

JAMIE'S DAD. Calm down, I'm here aren't I? Cheryl needed help 'round the house.

MARGARET. You? Helping 'round the house?! I've got to hand it to her, *Cheryl*, I could never make you lift a finger.

JAMIE'S DAD. What can I say, I'm a changed man.

MARGARET. Yeah. And I'm Angelina Jolie. So what would Cheryl say if she knew you were here with me?

JAMIE'S DAD. She'd kill me. Then you. Then herself. Probably in that order.

(*A moment of warmth between them.*)

MARGARET. Look. You're Jamie's dad, and he needs you, and I'm sick of covering.

JAMIE'S DAD. Right, his birthday –

MARGARET. I lied for you. Again. I picked out a card and said it came from you.
I even picked out a *crap* card, just like the sort of crap card you would have given him, plus twenty quid inside that I could not afford – Christ the lengths I go to for you!

JAMIE'S DAD. So stop then.

MARGARET. And tell him the truth! That his own dad can't be bothered to see him? Happy Birthday Jamie – surprise!

JAMIE'S DAD. Oh listen to yourself!

MARGARET. I wish you *would* listen! Jamie looked forward to his Saturdays with you – how long's it been since you spent time with him?

JAMIE'S DAD. No, don't you do that, Jamie *hated* Saturdays with me.

MARGARET. Cos you always dragged him off to the football! Couldn't you have done something Jamie would have liked for once?

JAMIE'S DAD. My Saturdays are *my* time – so if I want to go and support Wednesday on *my* day off –

MARGARET. It were never about football – it were about spending time with *you*!

JAMIE'S DAD. It were embarrassing! Me turning up at the match with...well you know what he's like!

MARGARET. You never commit to ow't! Like his bike that birthday. 'I'll teach him how to ride' you said, 'he's six now' – five minutes later he comes running back inside, in tears, you never bothered again. I had to teach him, just like I had to teach him *everything*!

JAMIE'S DAD. That were exactly what you wanted, don't you blame me for playing my part.

MARGARET. You're a crap dad – face it.

JAMIE'S DAD. Cos that's the part you gimme! We were young Margaret – Christ, we were still kids when we met. Stupid bloody kids – and I can't keep living in't past!

MARGARET. Who's living in the past? I'm not!

JAMIE'S DAD. What's this then?

> *(He takes hold of the gold locket 'round her neck.)*

MARGARET. What are you doing – get off!

JAMIE'S DAD. I bought you that necklace for your twenty-first.

MARGARET. Have you been drinking?

JAMIE'S DAD. I bought you that.

> (**MARGARET** *pulls away from him, holding the locket protectively.*)

MARGARET. You *have* been drinking. I don't suppose Cheryl's met him yet, has she? The one who comes in stinking of booze!

JAMIE'S DAD. She knows I like a drink, now't wrong with that.

MARGARET. First thing in't morning? Hid in your coffee? It's that smell, coffee and whisky, oh it takes me back!

JAMIE'S DAD. You must have been glad to see the back of me.

MARGARET. I was.

JAMIE'S DAD. Then why do you still wear it?

> (*He points to the locket.* **MARGARET** *stares at him, no answer.*)

Stop living in't past Mags. You can't keep hanging on to twenty-one. You can't keep hanging on to me.

MARGARET. I can't keep covering for you!

JAMIE'S DAD. Then stop! Tell him the truth! I am *done*. And that's what I came to tell you: Cheryl's pregnant.

> (**MARGARET** *stares at him, lost for words.*)

This time – it's planned, and it's what I want. Jamie were a mistake. You *used* him to tie me down. Well not anymore. Cheryl and me, we're having a boy.

MARGARET. Good for you.

JAMIE'S DAD. A *real* boy.

MARGARET. Jamie *is* a real boy! How can you say that about your own son?!

JAMIE'S DAD. My son. You know what I think when I look at my son? I think...

> (*Beat.*)

I married *you* for *that*?

> (**MARGARET**'s *heart breaks again – she's floored by this.*)

Don't call me again. We're done.

(He walks away – and out of her life.)

MARGARET. 'Done'? What do you mean 'done'! You were *lucky* to have us!

[MUSIC NO. 05 'IF I MET MYSELF AGAIN']

(Beat.)

You were lucky to have us…

IF I MET MYSELF BACK THEN
I WONDER WHAT I'D SAY?
WOULD I TELL THAT SIMPLE WIDE-EYED GIRL THE
    TRUTH?
IF I MET MYSELF AGAIN
A CHILD WHO'D LOST HER WAY
WHO WAS JUST ABOUT TO PAY THE PRICE OF YOUTH

I'D TELL HER 'ONLY FOOLS RUSH IN AND THINK THE
    HEART CAN LEAD'
I'D TELL HER 'GROW A THICKER SKIN COS GIRL YOU'RE
    GONNA BLEED'
I'D TELL HER 'BLUE SKIES TURN TO GREY – THE ONLY
    QUESTION'S WHEN'

I'D MAKE HER SEE
HER FUTURE'S ME
IF I MET MYSELF AGAIN

IF I MET MYSELF AGAIN
I WONDER WHAT SHE'D SAY?
THAT LOVE-STRUCK GIRL WHO THOUGHT SHE WAS SO
    SMART
IF I WARNED HER OF THE MEN
THE ONES THAT GOT AWAY
AND WORSE, THE ONES THAT STAY AND BREAK YOUR
    HEART

I'D TELL HER 'LOVE'S A LOSING GAME THAT'S BETTER
    LEFT UN-PLAYED'
I'D TELL HER 'YOU'VE YOURSELF TO BLAME FOR EV'RY
    CHOICE YOU'VE MADE!'
AN' I'D TELL HER –
AN' I'D TELL HER
'TIL MY VOICE GAVE OUT AND THEN –

MARGARET.

> SHE WOULD SMILE
> AND WAIT A WHILE,
> THEN GO AND DO IT ALL AGAIN
>
> IF I MET MYSELF AGAIN
>
> IF I MET THAT GIRL AGAIN I'D TELL HER 'SINK OR SWIM'!
> I'D WAKE HER UP AND GOD I'D MAKE HER RUN!
> I'D TURN BACK TIME AND SAY: 'GIRL STAY AWAY FROM
>   HIM!'
>
> BUT IF I DID,
> IF I DARED,
> THERE'S A PRICE
> I WOULD PAY
> AND I'D LOSE
>
> COS I WON'T
> HAVE MY SON
> IF I MET MYSELF AGAIN
>
> IF I MET MYSELF AGAIN...
>
> IF I MET MYSELF AGAIN...

6. Jamie's House

(**MARGARET** *doing the ironing.* **RAY** *lets herself in with her own key.*)

RAY. Cooee! Only me!

MARGARET. Ey up!

RAY. Here, present, half price, pound shop – bargain or what?

(*She hands* **MARGARET** *a cheap-looking box of chocolates.*)

MARGARET. 'After Sevens'?

RAY. Half price. Pound shop. Beggars can't be. And I got Jamie some lippie. Apparently it's the one Paris Hilton wears when she's shopping at Aldi.

(*She takes in* **MARGARET**'s *expression.*)

Well hello old friend.

MARGARET. You what?

RAY. That look on your face – ohhh, I know that look of old. Used to see it what – once, twice a week – whenever he'd done whatever it was he'd done to you. You've seen him haven't you?

MARGARET. Shhh, Jamie's upstairs.

RAY. His music's full blast, he won't hear n'owt 'cept Britney. So, go on, what's he said this time?

MARGARET. He's said...he's said he wants n'owt to do with Jamie.

RAY. I think we guessed that after Jamie's birthday. I'm sorry my love but that card fooled no one. Except Jamie, bless his soul.

MARGARET. Why can't he see him like *I* do...

(*Beat.*)

Cheryl's pregnant.

(**RAY** *lets this sink in.*)

RAY. Well that's it then. We'll never see him again. There's only one thing for it Mags – it's time to tell Jamie the truth. His dad don't want him.

(She stares at **MARGARET**. **MARGARET** *stares back.)*

(And then – **JAMIE** *bursts in, wearing his school uniform from the waist up, and the black sequin hot pants and his birthday heels from the waist down.)*

JAMIE. Guess what!! Guess what!! Guess what!! Guess what!! Guess what!! Guess what!! Guess what!! Guess what!!

*(***RAY** *looks him up and down.)*

RAY. You've done your hair different.

JAMIE. Oh ha ha! No – I've got news!

(Gives a twirl.)

By the way – what do you think?

RAY. Very nice. Brings out your...*eyes.*

MARGARET. How are you getting on in them heels son?

JAMIE. Oh I'm like an old pro. Go on – ask us to do anything. Anything at all.

MARGARET. Uh, okay, fetch us the brown sauce for the table will you love?

*(***JAMIE** *strides across the room to the sideboard where the sauces are, utterly confident and wobble-free.)*

JAMIE. Own brand or Daddies?

MARGARET. Oh, own brand. It's not been a Daddies day.

JAMIE. Ta-dah! Et voila!

(He deposits the sauce on the table with a flourish.)

RAY. I got this for you cookie. Lipstick. Apparently, it's the one Paris Hilton wears when she's shopping at Aldi.

JAMIE. 'Electric Lime & Kamikaze Kiwi'. Wow Ray, that's so sophisticated!

MARGARET. So go on then love – what's your news?

JAMIE. ...Mummy,

MARGARET. Uh-oh!

JAMIE. Can I borrow some money?

MARGARET. Not this month Jamie love.

JAMIE. Right. Only I've been saving up and there's that twenty quid from Dad but I'm still fifty short. Cos I've got it on loan for the night but it's so I can own it after.

MARGARET. Own what?

JAMIE. *(Beat.)* Me show dress.

> *(Silence.)*

Yeah. I said show dress. Mum, Ray...I've booked my first drag show!

MARGARET. No!

JAMIE. I have!

RAY. Chuffing Hell! How'd you do that?!

JAMIE. Well I googled this drag queen shop, for my prom dress –

MARGARET. Your prom dress!

JAMIE. My prom dress, cos doing the drag show is like the warm-up for the prom.

MARGARET. The prom!

JAMIE. The prom! Yes Mum, keep up! It's all part of making her *her*, building her, road testing her for the prom itself – well go on then, say something!

MARGARET. I don't know what *to* say.

JAMIE. Tell me I'm stupid. Tell me not to bother!

> *(Pause.)*

MARGARET. No I'm not going to say that. I'm going to say...

> *(Beat.)*

Do it. Just do it. Just go for it and...just ruddy do it.

JAMIE. Really?

MARGARET. Go to town. Be the most beautiful drag queen that prom's ever seen. Give the boys boners they won't know what to do with.

JAMIE. Mum!

MARGARET. I mean it! You live once – and that's it. You're living your life Jamie. I'm proud of you for it.

JAMIE. Oh my God! I'm doing it! I'm really doing it! I just need to pick a name.

MARGARET. What's wrong with your name?

JAMIE. Oh mum – do you know nothing about divergent gender identities? You have to become someone else – a drag queen in't just a boy in a dress!

RAY. Says who?

JAMIE. Says Loco Chanelle, and she knows cos she's had it all!

RAY. Loco who?

JAMIE. Oh Ray – the ignorance of yer! Everyone knows Loco Chanelle! She's like the most famous drag queen ever! After Our Lady RuPaul of course.

(Prays.) I'm sorry, you didn't hear me say that.

MARGARET. So you're going to prom, but not as yourself?

JAMIE. Yes, no, well – as a new me! A better me! I'm an event! I'm an artiste! Look all you want but don't touch what you can't afford.

RAY. So she's a people person then this drag queen of yours?

JAMIE. Shut up, you know what I mean. I just want to bring a bit of...glamour. To their otherwise dull grey lives. Like the Wizard of Oz. Sheffield were black and white – enter moi – and now it's Technicolor!

RAY. Oi you – our lives are not dull *or* grey.

JAMIE. Well that's cos you've got me around! Honestly, you'd all be lost without me and my Beyoncé walk.

(He struts up and down the front room, Beyoncé-style, getting very steady on his heels now.)

Mum... What would you say if I invited Dad to my drag show?

(*RAY stares at* **MARGARET**. *Her big chance to finally tell the truth.*)

MARGARET. I'll ask him. I need to talk to him anyway.

(**RAY** *scowls at* **MARGARET**.)

JAMIE. My first proper job...can you imagine, if he was there, *seeing* me...he might actually be proud.

(*Beat.*)

Right, I'm gonna go call Pritti and tell her about the show. Laters!

(*He runs into the hall and up the stairs.*)

MARGARET. Mind your heels on them stairs –

(*Crash!* **JAMIE** *tumbles over.*)

JAMIE. Ow! I'm alright! I'm alright! Weak ankles!

(*He picks himself up and limps the rest of the way upstairs.* **RAY** *yells up after him:*)

RAY. You're like a prodigy you are, you're Mozart in heels.

MARGARET. Look at him, in his first ever hot pants. He's becoming a man.

(*They laugh.*)

[MUSIC NO. 05A 'SCENE CHANGE']

7. Mayfield School: Corridor With Toilet

(A nondescript corridor leading between classrooms. At one end is the door to the disabled loos. **PRITTI**, *lost in her own little world, bumps into* **BEX**, **BECCA**, **FATIMAH** *and* **VICKI**.*)*

FATIMAH. Pritti – you got your prom ticket yet?

PRITTI. No, sorry.

VICKI. *Everyone's* coming! Please tell me you've heard about the dress code?

PRITTI. No. What is it?

VICKI, FATIMAH, BEX & BECCA. *Promfabulous.*

PRITTI. What does that mean?

FATIMAH. Like fairytale, like glamour, like Disney does Dior –

PRITTI. I don't think that sounds very me.

VICKI. Fatimah's Muslim, she's going.

FATIMAH. Wear something prommy, Allah don't mind a bit of sparkle, long as you cover up.

VICKI. Get a nice scarf. Stick a bit of tinsel on it.

FATIMAH. That's a juxtaposition. What? We did it in English!

VICKI. No – it's an oxymoron.

FATIMAH. No – *you're* an oxymoron.

PRITTI. Yeah, maybe, I'll think about it.

BECCA. Look at the time! Get a wriggle on, I've got detention in half an hour.

BEX. What did you do now?

BECCA. It were that sex education class with Mr Jennings. I kept correcting him.

> *(Giggling, the* **GIRLS** *exit. Then* **PRITTI** *hears through the disabled loo door:)*

JAMIE. *(Through door.)* Pssssst! Pritti! Pritti! Is that you?

PRITTI. Jamie?

JAMIE. *(Through door.)* Quick – get in here.

PRITTI. But I've got maths revision...

JAMIE. *(Through door.)* Come on! Please!

> *(He opens the door and pulls* **PRITTI** *inside. The disabled loo is a small room with a toilet, sink and a mirror with a small window above it.)*
>
> *(***JAMIE** *is trying to do his makeup for the first time in it and he has been painting on eyebrows. They are completely different shapes, heights and thicknesses.)*

PRITTI. Jamie! What are you doing!

JAMIE. Look! Just look at my eyebrows! It's like my forehead's being stabbed by epileptic caterpillars!

PRITTI. Did you do that yourself?

JAMIE. No Pritti, I'm the victim of a drive-by clowning – yes of course I did it myself! I've been trying to get it right but eyebrows are my Achilles heel! Please help me – I can't become my inner drag queen if I can't even do her outer eyebrows!

PRITTI. Jamie – I've got maths revision.

JAMIE. Pritti! My eyebrows!

PRITTI. Jamie, I've got maths revision so I can pass my exams so I can go to Cambridge so I can become a doctor!

JAMIE. Yes, but this is *important*! Oh God – who is she though? Is she good? Bad? Fun? Bitchy? Maybe she's a killer, maybe she's a kleptomaniac, maybe she murdered a man for this lash-lengthening mascara – I just don't know!

PRITTI. God knows why you're asking me to help – I never wear makeup.

JAMIE. Well, that's cos you don't need to because you're so pretty.

PRITTI. No, my *name* is Pritti. I think my parents were being ironic.

JAMIE. Pritti – please!

PRITTI. Ugh! Give it here – look at me. I don't know what I'm doing.

JAMIE. The show's *tonight* and I'm running out of time! You are coming aren't you?

PRITTI. I can't – my dad's forbid it. He says you're a bad influence and I've got to stay in my room.

JAMIE. So just climb out the window!

PRITTI. Yeah, see that's the kind of bad influence he's talking about.

> (*Bang bang bang!* MISS HEDGE *is standing outside the disabled loo, banging on the door.*)

MISS HEDGE. What's going on in there!

JAMIE. Bloody hell! Miss Hedge! She mustn't see me like this! Hide me!

PRITTI. There isn't anywhere!

JAMIE. Find somewhere!

PRITTI. What am I s'posed to do – flush you?!

MISS HEDGE. This is your final warning, I'm unlocking this door.

> (*She takes out a master key, opens the door.*)

JAMIE. Give me a leggie out the window!

> (*He scrambles towards the small, high window – but it's hopeless –* MISS HEDGE *enters to find* PRITTI *standing there in a panic, and* JAMIE *wedged halfway through the window, his back to her, his arse sticking out.*)

MISS HEDGE. Who does that backside belong to?

> (*Pause.*)

JAMIE. ...Me Miss.

MISS HEDGE. Jamie New. Surprise surprise. *And* Pritti Pasha – I'm disappointed in you, getting led astray into... What is it you're doing in here?

(*Pause.* **JAMIE***'s arse is still the only thing we can see of him.*)

JAMIE. ...Parkour Miss.

MISS HEDGE. What?

JAMIE. You know, free running. It went wrong.

MISS HEDGE. Jamie New – get down here!

(**JAMIE** *gets down, consciously keeping his face turned away from* **MISS HEDGE.**)

Turn around and face me.

(*Pause.*)

JAMIE. ...No, you're alright Miss.

MISS HEDGE. Turn around and face me *now*.

(*Slowly,* **JAMIE** *turns, revealing his poorly made-up face.*)

Well, this is certainly an escalation from nail varnish isn't it Jamie?

(*Pause.* **JAMIE** *trying to work out what to say. Then:*)

PRITTI. It's an art project Miss. I'm exploring...gender identity. I wanted to use a face as a canvas to make a statement. But I'm not very good at eyebrows.

JAMIE. She's not.

MISS HEDGE. So why aren't you doing this in the art department?

(*Pause.*)

PRITTI. Jamie's shy.

JAMIE. I am.

(**MISS HEDGE** *stares at him, trying to work this out.*)

MISS HEDGE. Why do you try so hard to make things difficult for yourself?

JAMIE. I don't Miss. I don't know what you mean.

MISS HEDGE. Art project…if you say so Pritti, I'll believe you. But I think you should go back to the art department to finish the…'piece' off.

JAMIE. Right, I'll just wash off my face and –

MISS HEDGE. – What are you saying Jamie! You're Pritti's work of art! You can't just wash a work of art down the drain! That's an act of vandalism. Go as you are.

JAMIE. Please Miss, don't.

[MUSIC NO. 06 'WORK OF ART']

*(As the opening plays, **MISS HEDGE** leads **JAMIE** and **PRITTI** out of the loo. This is **JAMIE***'s *long walk of shame – everyone pointing and laughing at him.)*

MISS HEDGE. The corridors are your catwalk Jamie, the students; your audience. I want the entire school to see this. Your public awaits.

YOU BELONG IN THE SPOTLIGHT
ON THE WALL OF THE TATE
IN A TEN-MEGAWATT LIGHT
COS YOUR BRUSHWORK'S SO GREAT!

YOU'RE THE NEXT PHASE IN FEMININE
YOU'RE A LICHTENSTEIN DOT
YOU'RE A BED WITH TRACEY EMIN IN
YOU'RE GRAYSON PERRY'S NEXT POT

WORK OF ART
WORK OF ART
YOU'RE A PERFECT WORK OF ART
MONA LISA
THIS IS SHE, SIR
WITH A SMILE TO MELT YOUR HEART
WORK OF ART
WORK OF ART
YOU'RE A PERFECT WORK OF ART
LIKE PICASSO
SO KICK ASS, OH

I JUST DON'T KNOW WHERE TO START!
WORK OF ART
WORK OF ART

YOU'RE YOKO ONO ON VINYL

DEAN.

OH YOU JUST RAISED THE BAR

MISS HEDGE.

YOU'RE A CANVAS THAT'S BLANK

DEAN.

WATCH YOUR VALUE INCREASE

MISS HEDGE.

YOU'RE A DUCHAMP URINAL

DEAN.

SEE HOW PRECIOUS YOU ARE!

MISS HEDGE.

YOU'RE HALF A DEAD COW IN A TANK

DEAN.

YOU'RE THE SCHOOL MASTERPIECE!

KIDS (EXCEPT JAMIE).

WORK OF ART
WORK OF ART
YOU'RE A PERFECT WORK OF ART
MONA LISA
THIS IS SHE, SIR
WITH A SMILE TO MELT YOUR HEART
WORK OF ART
WORK OF ART
YOU'RE A PERFECT WORK OF ART
LIKE PICASSO
SO KICK ASS, OH
I JUST DON'T KNOW WHERE TO START!
WORK OF ART

MISS HEDGE. I'm teaching you a lesson Jamie. I told you all; your best chance at life was to keep things real, but there's always one who thinks I don't mean them. And surprise surprise Jamie New – it's you; the work of art. But a work of art is nothing if it's not put on show Jamie –

DEAN. So go on then – put on a show.

MISS HEDGE. The lights – the glamour –

DEAN. The centre of attention –

MISS HEDGE. This is it Jamie. I hope it's everything you've ever wanted.

JAMIE. This is *everything* I ever wanted. My stage – my audience – my dancers – all eyes on ME!

>*(He gestures – and the **KIDS** lift **MISS HEDGE** up and whisk her offstage, on **JAMIE**'s command. **JAMIE** stares at **DEAN**.)*

You wanna look? Keep looking! I'll be in drag tonight, at Legs Eleven, so come along – if you dare!

DEAN. You're just a boy in a dress!

JAMIE. Oh Dean, a boy in a dress is something to be laughed at – but a drag queen is something to be feared.

AND *I AM A DRAG QUEEN*!

KIDS (GROUP 1).

>YES YOU ARE
>YES YOU ARE
>YES YOU ARE OH

KIDS (GROUP 2).

>YOU'RE THE BIZ
>YOU'RE THE BIZ
>YOU'RE THE BIZ YEAH

KIDS (GROUP 1).

>SUPERSTAR
>SUPERSTAR
>SUPERSTAR OH

KIDS (GROUP 2).

>YOU'RE THE SHIZ
>YOU'RE THE – SHIZ, THE SHIZ YEAH

KIDS (GROUP 1).

>YOU'RE SO NEAT
>YOU'RE SO NEAT
>YOU'RE SO NEAT YO

KIDS (GROUP 2).
OFF THE CHART
OFF THE – CHART, THE CHART YEAH

KIDS (GROUP 1).
SUPER SWEET
SUPER SWEET
SUPER SWEET OH

KIDS (GROUP 2).
WORK OF ART
WORK OF ART
WORK OF ART YEAH

KIDS (GROUPS 1 & 2).
WORK OF ART
WORK OF ART
WORK OF ART YEAH

KIDS (GROUPS 1 & 2) & JAMIE.
WORK OF ART
WORK OF ART

JAMIE.
YES, I AM A WORK OF ART!
YOU WON'T SHAME ME
YOU SHOULD FRAME ME
I'M A JAMIE WORK OF ART!

KIDS (GROUPS 1 & 2) & JAMIE.
WORK OF ART
WORK OF ART

JAMIE.
GONNA BLOW YOUR WORLD APART
I'M OFFENDING
I'M A TRENDING
GENDER-BENDING
GENDER-BLENDING
GENDER-PENDING
GENDER-ENDING
AND TRANSCENDING

KIDS (GROUPS 1 & 2) & JAMIE.
WORK OF ART!

[MUSIC NO. 06A 'WORK OF ART (PLAYOFF)']

8. Outside Legs Eleven

(Legs Eleven is a fun – if not massively sophisticated-looking – drag club. Three **DRAG QUEENS** *exit, getting some air.* **LAIKA VIRGIN, TRAY SOPHISTICAY** *and* **SANDRA BOLLOCK.***)*

LAIKA VIRGIN. Look at me – I'm bricking it. Imagine getting stage fright at my age. Twenty-one.

TRAY SOPHISTICAY. I thought you were twenty-one your last birthday.

SANDRA BOLLOCK. And the one before that.

LAIKA VIRGIN. I'm always twenty-one. That's how I'm so good at it.

SANDRA BOLLOCK. I know why you're so nervous. It's because *she's* back.

TRAY SOPHISTICAY. Tell me about it! The last time she touched her toes on that stage, I was a drag embryo.

SANDRA BOLLOCK. It's gonna be a night to remember. Like your twenty-first. And your twenty-first. And your twenty-first.

LAIKA VIRGIN. You're just jealous of my youthful beauty. Talentless queen.

SANDRA BOLLOCK. Talentless? They call me Helen of Troy cos my face could launch a thousand ships.

TRAY SOPHISTICAY. They call you Helen of Troy cos you look like a horse. Oh heck, is that the time, we've gotta do our warmup!

(They each take a deep breath, as if they're about to do a vocal warm-up...but instead they all let out a loud burp.)

DRAG QUEENS. *Aaaaaand RELAX!*

SANDRA BOLLOCK. That's better, now I feel like a professional.

(They re-enter the club, slamming the door behind them.)

(JAMIE appears, carrying his red dress, full of nerves. He heads to the door – when DEAN saunters up, super casual.)

DEAN. Alright Jamie.

JAMIE. Dean? What are you doing here?

DEAN. Come to see your show, an't I? There's a load of us, from school, all come to see it. Like you said.

JAMIE. Why?

DEAN. Why do you think?

JAMIE. Dunno.

(Beat.)

To show your support?

DEAN. Thing is... I knew you were gay. But I didn't know you were some ladyboy as well.

JAMIE. Drag queen!

DEAN. FREAKSHOW. That's what you are!

JAMIE. Dean Paxton, find a brick wall and run into it, do us all a favour.

DEAN. You think you're bulletproof you, don't you – but I know the bullet. I know the word.

JAMIE. Yeah yeah – gay sissy queer boy.

DEAN. *Minger.* You're a minger.

JAMIE. I'm not.

DEAN. You put on a wig, and makeup, and a dress – and you look like a *minger*. Like an ugly boy in ugly girls' ugly clothes. A dirty, ugly *minger*. And you know it. And we know it. And we'll all be out there to tell you about it. So – break a leg. Ta-ra.

(DEAN slinks away, leaving JAMIE shellshocked.)

[MUSIC NO. 06B 'SCENE CHANGE']

9. Legs Eleven

(Backstage at the club. The dressing room is empty, but full of clothes and makeup, like it's about to burst into life. **MARGARET** *and* **RAY** *appear, both in their best clothes, fishes out of water.* **RAY** *picks up a large, padded sequin bra with tassels, gives the tassels a twirl.)*

RAY. Toto, we're not in ASDA anymore.

*(**LAIKA VIRGIN** enters, on the phone, doing a deep voice.)*

LAIKA VIRGIN. You wanna pick a fight with *me* sunbeam I says to him, I'll knock you seven shades of pink into the middle of next –

(He sees **RAY** *and* **MARGARET,** *and his voice becomes ladylike and goes up an octave or two.)*

– hiya ladies.

MARGARET & RAY. Hiya.

LAIKA VIRGIN. Welcome to Legs Eleven, hope you're feeling the fantasy.

*(**TRAY SOPHISTICAY** enters.)*

RAY. Look at the legs on him! I'm well jell.

MARGARET. Excuse me. *Excuse me.* I'm Jamie New's mum, we're looking for –

SANDRA BOLLOCK. – Jamie! Oh we love Jamie, makes us all feel ancient though dun't he, shiny little high-kicking foetus that he is, but he's a tribute to you Margaret. And you must be Ray. We've heard all about you. *All* about you. Now there's someone waiting for you in the VIP room.

MARGARET. The VIP room!

SANDRA BOLLOCK. Hunty! You've got company!

LOCO CHANELLE. *(Offstage.)* Coming!

(The sound of a cistern flushing.)

RAY. The VIP room...

LOCO CHANELLE. *(Offstage.)* Are you Brazilian, six foot two and a heavily tattooed sailor?

MARGARET & RAY. ...No.

LOCO CHANELLE. *(Offstage.)* Damn you all to hell, I'm coming in anyways.

> *(And **LOCO CHANELLE** sashays onto the stage – an older stateswoman of a drag queen, a Kathleen Turner-style creation, fierce as hell, not an ounce of sentimentality but full of tough love.)*

MARGARET. Hello. I'm Margaret, Jamie's mum.

RAY. And I'm Ray.

LOCO CHANELLE. Oh – I know who *you* are. Perhaps my legend precedes me also. I'm Miss Loco Chanelle. Mwah, mwah, please sit!

RAY. Loco Chanelle? Hang on, aren't you the most famous drag queen what ever lived?

> *(**LOCO CHANELLE** gestures to her humble surroundings.)*

LOCO CHANELLE. Clearly. Now pay attention, it's time you met the girls. They're the best that money can buy when you're on a budget. This is the legendary Laika Virgin –

LAIKA VIRGIN. Hiya ladies, looking gorgeous.

LOCO CHANELLE. Miss Tray Sophisticay –

TRAY SOPHISTICAY. *Tracey* Sophisticay, thank you, I'm what we call 'a class act'.

LOCO CHANELLE. Indeed she is, as are we all, and this is Sandra Bollock.

> *(**SANDRA BOLLOCK** turns, in the process of adjusting her crutch.)*

SANDRA BOLLOCK. Owright.

(MARGARET and RAY just gape, overwhelmed.)

LOCO CHANELLE. Look at us, all girls together. Well I say 'girls' – I do have one small secret of my own. *(Stage whisper.) I'm not a natural red head.* Now, where is our precious precocious little Jamie, he's not chickening out I hope?

MARGARET. I thought he were here already.

TRAY SOPHISTICAY. Should've been here twenty minutes ago.

LAIKA VIRGIN. Typical girl, fashionably late.

SANDRA BOLLOCK. Typical boy, terrible timekeeper.

TRAY SOPHISTICAY. That's the problem with us – we're the worst of both worlds!

LAIKA VIRGIN. Hey, will you shut that door, that breeze is freezing me nips off, and these tits are out of warranty.

TRAY SOPHISTICAY. Are those tits hunty? I thought you'd put your buttocks on backwards. Hang on – here she is!

(JAMIE enters, carrying his dress and shoes.)

MARGARET. Oh Jamie, there's someone here who wants to meet you.

(MARGARET gestures to LOCO CHANELLE, but JAMIE doesn't even look.)

JAMIE. No, I can't go on, Mum.

MARGARET. What?

RAY. Jamie!

JAMIE. I can't.

MARGARET. Jamie,

JAMIE. No Mum!

MARGARET. Jamie, just turn 'round.

(JAMIE looks 'round – and sees LOCO CHANELLE for the first time. LOCO smiles and waves.)

LOCO CHANELLE. Hello sailor. The name's Loco Chanelle.

JAMIE. ...Hugo?

LOCO CHANELLE. Hugo? Hugo who? Who's this 'Hugo', I
   dunno, he sounds fabulous,

JAMIE. I'm sorry, but I can't go on, Dean Paxton and his
   mates are here from school.

LOCO CHANELLE. I couldn't give a pixie's poop about Dean
   Paxton! Jamie New, I risked life, limb and possible
   incarceration to return to public life for one night only,
   and do you know why? So that I can introduce your
   good self onto my great stage. Don't you dare tell me it's
   been a wasted journey!

JAMIE. You're not listening! I haven't even got a drag queen
   name figured out! I'm pathetic! I'm sorry but I can't go
   on.

LOCO CHANELLE. Girls, a moment.

   (The DRAG QUEENS *start to file out.)*

Ladies, if you'd be so kind.

   (She gestures – she means RAY *and* MARGARET
   too.)

MARGARET. Good luck love.

RAY. Break a nail.

   (The DRAG QUEENS *and* MARGARET *and* RAY
   exit. A silence descends in the dressing room.)

LOCO CHANELLE. Newsflash Jamie, it's called stage fright.
   Own it and deal with it.

JAMIE. He says there's a load of them, come to take the
   mickey and...he's right, I'm just a stupid ugly minger.

LOCO CHANELLE. *(Gasps!)* We do *not* use the M word in
   here! The drag queen you're gonna be; her power, her
   fearlessness, her anger – she's your bulletproof vest.

JAMIE. Then who is she?! I can't see her. I can't find her!

LOCO CHANELLE. So she won't come to you? Fine. You
   go to her. Out there on that stage, that's where she is
   kiddo – your best friend, ready and waiting, so suck it
   up and go say hello!

JAMIE. But I've got no name, I've got no backstory – I've got no eyebrows!

LOCO CHANELLE. Good God – *we'll* do your eyebrows, *we'll* make you look beautiful, and you can borrow some tits from the tit box!

[MUSIC NO. 07 'OVER THE TOP']

Just you think about who you are, and who you want to be.

WHEN THE DOGS OF WAR ARE DANCING
AND THE ARROWS HIT THEIR MARK
WHEN YOUR DAYS ARE GETTING DARKER
WHEN THERE'S DAGGERS IN THE DARK

YOU WILL ALWAYS FIND YOUR SPOTLIGHT
YOU WILL ALWAYS FIND YOUR FEET
SCREAM UNTIL YOUR LUNGS EXPIRE
READY, STEADY, AIM AND FIRE!

DID YOU THINK IT WOULD BE EASY?
YOU'RE ONE FOOTSTEP FROM DEFEAT
BUT A SOLDIER SHAN'T SURRENDER
AND A HERO CAN'T RETREAT

THOUGH YOUR ENEMY SURROUNDS YOU
AND THEY'VE GOT YOU IN THEIR SIGHTS
SOUND THE BUGLES!

(**TRAY, LAIKA** *and* **SANDRA** *bustle back in.*)

DRAG QUEENS.
ALL SET SARGE!

LOCO CHANELLE, TENORS & BASSES.
READY, STEADY, AIM AND CHARGE!

OVER THE TOP, MY FRIEND
UNTO THE BREACH MY FRIEND
REND THE UNENDING NIGHT
LET'S GET YOUR ARMOUR ON
LET'S GET YOUR WAR PAINT DONE

LOCO CHANELLE.	**DRAG QUEENS.**
COS IT'S TIME TO FIGHT	HOO!

> *(LAIKA exits. LOCO commands JAMIE:)*

LOCO CHANELLE. Right Jamie, strip! Auntie Tray, tell Jamie your Top Tip for Tackling Terrible Stage Fright.

TRAY SOPHISTICAY. Pleasure treasure: right, when you get out on that stage, take a good long look at that audience, and try to imagine them all –

JAMIE. – Naked.

TRAY SOPHISTICAY. Naked? I was gonna say 'dead' but whatever floats your boat.

> *(LAIKA VIRGIN enters, carrying a bouquet of flowers.)*

LAIKA VIRGIN. Flower delivery at stage door! As I always say: everything's okay with a bouquet.

LOCO CHANELLE. A gift to welcome Loco Chanelle back into the fold? Oh, I am blushing!

LAIKA VIRGIN. Sorry Ms Mutton – these are for Lady Lamb – card says 'Jamie New'.

JAMIE. Flowers? No! That's mental!

> *(He reads the card.)*

'Your mum told me about the show, and I'm sorry I can't be there, but thanks for the invite. Good luck son. Dad.' It's from me dad! 'P.s. The dress is paid for.'

LOCO CHANELLE. Oh – I'd forget my own head if it wasn't so damned fabulous. There was an envelope pushed through the door of Victor's Secret this morning from a Mr New – that must be your dad, lucky you kiddo – it's been a long time since I've had such a generous daddy.

JAMIE. Dad paid for...! No!

LOCO CHANELLE. And he paid cash – the dress is yours. Not just for tonight you hear me? Yours forever.

JAMIE. I can't believe it!

> *(He stares at his flowers, and makes his decision.)*

This is for you, Dad!

(The **DRAG QUEENS** *whoop in response!)*

LOCO CHANELLE.	LAIKA, TRAY, SANDRA & OFFSTAGE ENSEMBLE.
WHEN YOUR SISTERS ARE BEHIND YOU	AHH-OO!
THEY'RE YOUR BROTHERS MARCHING TOO	LEFT TURN
THEN THE WARRIOR WITHIN YOU	AHH-OO!
COMES TO RUN THE DRAGON THROUGH!	RIGHT TURN!
THOUGH YOUR DARKEST DEMON COMES THE DAY THAT YOU DOUBT	
YOU'LL BECOME A HE-MAN, EV'RY DEMON YOU ROUT	
TIME TO FACE YOUR FEAR	
	YOUR FEAR
READY, STEADY, AIM AND CHEER!	

LOCO CHANELLE & OFFSTAGE ENSEMBLE.

OVER THE TOP, MY FRIEND.

LAIKA, TRAY & SANDRA.

QUICK STEP, FORWARD MARCH, LEFT TURN, RIGHT HOOK.

LOCO CHANELLE & OFFSTAGE ENSEMBLE.

UNTO THE BREACH MY FRIEND.

LAIKA, TRAY & SANDRA.

CLEAN SHOES, FRESH STARCH, OLD DOG, NEW LOOK.

LOCO CHANELLE & OFFSTAGE ENSEMBLE.

REND THE UNENDING NIGHT.

LAIKA, TRAY & SANDRA.

WE SHALL FIGHT THEM ON THE BEACHES!

LOCO CHANELLE & OFFSTAGE ENSEMBLE.

YOU'VE GOT YOUR ARMOUR ON.

**LOCO CHANELLE, LAIKA, TRAY, SANDRA
& OFFSTAGE ENSEMBLE.**

YOU'VE HAD YOUR WARPAINT DONE
AND YOU'LL BE A MAN, MY SON!

LOCO CHANELLE.	**LAIKA, TRAY & SANDRA.**
SO GET OUT THERE AND FIGHT!	HOO!

It's time Jamie – name her!
Who is she?! Who is she?!

JAMIE. I don't know!	HOO!

LOCO. You *have* to know!

JAMIE. I don't know!

LOCO. Come on! What's all of this	HOO!
about?!	

JAMIE. I don't –

LOCO. – You *do*!	HOO!

JAMIE. I can't –

LOCO. Say it Jamie! Say it!

JAMIE. It's about me! Me! ME!!!	HOO!

(**LOCO** *grins at him.*)

LOCO. That's *it* kiddo!

(*Blackout.*)

(**LOCO***'s voice crackles over the sound system:*)

LOCO CHANELLE. Ladies and Gentlemen – would you
please welcome onto the Legs Eleven stage, for her
premiere appearance, her virgin unveiling, her maiden
voyage – the soon to be legendary...*MISS MIMI ME!*

[MUSIC NO. 08 'OUT OF THE DARKNESS']

(*And suddenly we're in full-on backstage
world as the lights come on again, revealing*
JAMIE *waiting nervously behind a large,
sparkly curtain, the unseen audience and
club on the blind side.* **TRAY SOPHISTICAY** *and*
LAIKA VIRGIN *hurry to do* **JAMIE***'s finishing
touches – putting on his wig and the last*

flourishes of makeup – as **SANDRA BOLLOCK** *parades 'round carrying a light-up chaser board that announces the name of the newest drag queen in town: 'MIMI ME' – showing it off to the unseen, imagined club audience [and our actual 'backstage' audience so that the pun lands] like a glamour girl at a big fight.)*

(And then, from beyond the curtain, we hear the build of two competing sounds: the rising pulse of the intro to the prerecorded version of 'Out of the Darkness' – and the rising chant of 'Minger, minger, minger' – led by an unseen **DEAN** *and his mates.)*

GIRLS.

OUT OF THE DARKNESS
INTO THE SPOTLIGHT

BOYS.

MINGER, MINGER,

GIRLS.

OUT OF THE DARKNESS

BOYS.

MINGER,

GIRLS.

INTO THE SPOTLIGHT

BOYS.

MINGER, MINGER, MINGER, MINGER, MINGER

(The song builds, builds, builds – the tension rising as **JAMIE** *fully metamorphoses into Mimi [but we don't reveal the full red dress just yet]......)*

(...And the **DRAG QUEENS** *part the curtains, holding them open as the bright lights of the club beyond blaze through, throwing* **JAMIE/ MIMI** *into silhouette...)*

*(...As **MIMI ME** strides through to meet her destiny on the other side.)*

(And the stage is plunged into black.)

End of Act One

ACT II

1. Mayfield School: Classroom

(We hear a school bell.)

[MUSIC NO. 09 'EVERYBODY'S TALKING ABOUT JAMIE']

*(All the kids, minus **JAMIE**, are gossiping excitedly in their classroom before the start of the lesson.)*

*(**BEX, BECCA, LEVI, SAYID, CY** and **PRITTI** all went to the show so are doing the telling. **FATIMAH, MICKEY** and **VICKI** didn't go, so are doing the listening and mixing up the second-hand story. **DEAN** also went, but refuses to join in so doesn't sing, sitting sullenly at the back.)*

BEX & BECCA.

YOU SHOULDA SEEN IT,
YOU SHOULDA BEEN THERE,
YOU WON'T BELIEVE THE STUFF WE SAW THAT WENT
    DOWN IN THERE.

BEX.

THE MEN WERE WOMEN,

BECCA.

THE GIRLS WERE FELLAS,

BEX & BECCA.

THEY DID A RAIN DANCE WEARING NOTHING BUT
    UMBRELLAS
PASS IT ON!

SAYID.

> THERE WAS A LADY,
> SHE HAD A SISTER,

LEVI.

> BUT IT WAS KINDA WEIRD THE WAY THE LADY KISSED
> HER.

CY.

> THERE WAS A WOMAN

LEVI.

> WHOSE NAME WAS NORMAN

CY.

> AND THE FRILLY KNICKERS –

BEX & BECCA.

> THAT WAS JUST THE DOORMAN!

BEX, BECCA, SAYID, LEVI & CY.

> PASS IT ON!

MICKEY.

> THERE WAS A DOORMAN
> WHOSE NAME WAS NORMAN
> AND THEN THE DOORMAN KISSED HIS SISTER

FATIMAH.

> SHE'S A MORMON
> I HEARD THERE'S DUNGEONS
> INSIDE THE CELLARS

VICKI.

> WHERE THEY RAIN DOWN PAIN AND SPANK YOU WITH
> UMBRELLAS!

ALL KIDS.

> EV'RYBODY'S TALKING 'BOUT JAMIE
> EV'RYBODY'S TALKING 'BOUT J-J-JAMIE
> EV'RYBODY'S TALKING 'BOUT THE BOY IN THE DRESS
> WHO WAS BORN TO IMPRESS
> EV'RYBODY'S TALKING 'BOUT THE THINGS THAT HE WORE
> EV'RYBODY LISTENING COS WE NEED TO KNOW MORE
> EV'RYBODY'S TALKING 'BOUT THE BOY IN THE WIG
> COS HE'S GONNA BE BIG!
> EV'RYBODY'S TALKING 'BOUT JAY-AY-AY-AY-MIE!

BEX.

AND THERE WAS MUSIC

BECCA.

AND THERE WAS DANCING

BEX & BECCA.

AND ALL THE DRAG QUEENS HAVE TO LIP-SYNC COS THEY
CAN'T SING.

PASS IT ON!

LEVI.

AND THERE WAS SMOKING

CY.

AND THERE WAS BOOZING

SAYID.

AND THERE WERE BOYS THAT LOOKED LIKE GIRLS
WHICH WAS CONFUSING

LEVI.

PASS IT ON!

VICKI.

SO WHAT'S A LIP-SYNC?

IS THAT LIKE KISSING?

MICKEY.

YEAH, HE KISSED A GIRL WHOSE GIRLIE PARTS WERE
MISSING.

ALL KIDS.

EV'RYBODY'S TALKING 'BOUT JAMIE

EV'RYBODY'S TALKING 'BOUT J-J-JAMIE

EV'RYBODY'S TALKING 'BOUT THE BOY ON THE STAGE

WHO BROKE OUT OF HIS CAGE!

EV'RYBODY'S TALKING 'BOUT THE SWITCH AND THE LIPS

EV'RYBODY'S TALKING 'BOUT THE TITS AND THE HIPS

EV'RYBODY'S TALKING 'BOUT THAT CRAZY KID

AND ALL THE THINGS THAT HE DID!

EV'RYBODY'S TALKING 'BOUT JAY-AY-AY-AY-MIE!

SAYID.

HE HAD ONE GO-GO BOY

SAYID & LEVI.

FIVE GO-GO BOYS

SAYID, LEVI & CY.

TEN GO-GO BOYS – IN KILTS

MICKEY, FATIMAH & VICKY.

IN KILTS!

BEX.

HE HAD ONE DANCING GIRL,

BEX & BECCA.

FIVE DANCING GIRLS,

BEX, BECCA & PRITTI.

TEN DANCING GIRLS – ON STILTS.

MICKEY, FATIMAH & VICKY.

ON STILTS!

SAYID, PRITTI & BECCA.

HE HAD ONE BACKING SINGER,

BECCA, SAYID, PRITTI & BEX.

FIVE BACKING SINGERS,

CY & PRITTI.

TEN BACKING SINGERS – PLUS CHOIR

MICKEY, FATIMAH & VICKY.

AAAAH AAAAH AAAAAH AAAAAAAAH!

BECCA & PRITTI.

HE DID ONE SOMERSAULT,

BEX, BECCA, PRITTI & SAYID.

FIVE SOMERSAULTS
TEN SOMERSAULTS –

ALL KIDS.

ON FIRE!
EV'RYBODY'S TALKING 'BOUT JAMIE
EV'RYBODY'S TALKING 'BOUT J-J-JAMIE
EV'RYBODY'S TALKING 'BOUT THE BUZZ FROM THE
   CROWD FOR THE BOY WHO WAS PROUD!
EV'RYBODY'S TALKING 'BOUT JAY-AY-AY-AY-MIE!

    (**MISS HEDGE** *enters and the class falls quiet,*
    underscore beneath her dialogue:)

MISS HEDGE. Alright Year Eleven, settle down, eyes front, I need to talk you through your exam timetables for the next few weeks...

> *(The* **KIDS** *keep going in whispers, and* **MISS HEDGE** *continues to drone on from the front.)*

BEX & BECCA. *(Whispering.)*
AND THERE WERE COCKTAILS,
AND THERE WERE MOCKTAILS

SAYID. *(Whispering.)*
SHE WORE A SCALY SKIRT SHE SAID WERE MADE OF CROCK TAILS

MISS HEDGE. ...Which means those of you doing history and geography will have a double exam that day –

LEVI & CY. *(Whispering.)*
AND THERE WERE FEATHERS
AND THERE WERE LEATHERS

SAYID. *(Whispering.)*
AND THERE WERE RUBBER GEAR SHE SAID WERE FOR ALL WEATHERS

MISS HEDGE. ...There is no such thing as 'time off' between exams – only revision time, which means – are you listening at the back?

BEX & BECCA. *(Whispering.)*
AND THERE WERE THIGH BOOTS

LEVI & CY.
AND THERE WERE HIGH BOOTS

SAYID. *(Whispering.)*
AND THERE WERE GIRL-BOOTS-THAT-YOU-WEAR-IF-YOU'RE-A-GUY-BOOTS

ALL KIDS. *(Variously, getting louder.)*
EV'RYBODY'S TALKING 'BOUT JAMIE
EV'RYBODY'S TALKING 'BOUT JAMIE
EV'RYBODY'S TALKING 'BOUT JAMIE
EV'RYBODY'S TALKING 'BOUT JAMIE
EV'RYBODY'S –

> (**MISS HEDGE** *yells at the class, and the music*
> *cuts out to silence!*)

MISS HEDGE. SHUT UP! For pity's sake Year Eleven! What's got into all of you? Pritti!

PRITTI. Yes Miss Hedge?

MISS HEDGE. What is going on?

PRITTI. ...Nothing Miss.

MISS HEDGE. No, the whole class is clearly up to something – so tell me please: what is everybody talking about?

> (**PRITTI** *looks 'round, crippled by shyness,*
> *then slowly draws the courage to open her*
> *mouth – and the music blasts back in.*)

PRITTI.
EV'RYBODY'S TALKING 'BOUT JAMIE
EV'RYBODY'S TALKING 'BOUT JAMIE
EV'RYBODY'S TALKING 'BOUT THE BOY IN THE DRESS
WHO WAS BORN TO EXPRESS!

GROUP 1.	GROUP 2.
EV'RYBODY'S TALKING AND WE'RE TALKING ABOUT	TALKING
THE EYES AND THE THIGHS AND THE PUH-PUH-PUH-POUT	EV'RYBODY'S TALKING
EV'RYBODY'S TALKING AND THERE AIN'T NO DOUBT	EV'RYBODY'S TALKING
WHO WE'RE DYING TO SEE!	AH

ALL KIDS.
EV'RYBODY'S TALKING 'BOUT JAY-AY-AY-AY-AY-AY-AY-MIE!

> (*The door bursts open – and* **JAMIE** *strides*
> *in, wearing OTT large sunglasses like Liz*
> *Taylor with a hangover, head wrapped up in*
> *a brightly-coloured scarf.*)

JAMIE. Hiya, is everybody talking about me?

MISS HEDGE. And where have you been Jamie New?

JAMIE. I had a late night Miss, overslept, sorry.

MISS HEDGE. No, I'm sorry Jamie. I'm sorry that you suddenly feel the need to be the centre of attention.

JAMIE. I don't know what you're talking about Miss.

> *(He removes his massive sunglasses, revealing that he's got sparkly eye makeup on and false lashes. The class gives a gasp of shocked delight!* **DEAN** *can't believe it.)*

DEAN. Miss!

MISS HEDGE. Jamie New – you know full well that makeup like that is completely against school uniform rules!

JAMIE. The school uniform rules for the *girls*, yes Miss, but if you check the code for the boys – *and I did* – it don't say nothing about makeup at all. Hiya Dean – you having a nice day so far?

MISS HEDGE. What have I told you about keeping it real?!

JAMIE. Oh who cares about *real*, Miss? Real's for little people, and you see this makeup? That's Mimi Me.

MISS HEDGE. It's Mimi-what?

JAMIE. Mimi Me. Me drag queen name. Mimi's a poor girl from the wrong side of town who's set her sights on becoming the future Mrs Prince Harry Of Hearts – nothing lasts forever Meghan – and it's all thanks to you Miss, testing me like you did. Cos now I really *am* your work of art.

> *(He sashays to his desk – utterly victorious. The bell goes.)*

MISS HEDGE. Right, well that is the end of your final lesson.

> *(Cheers from the* **KIDS***!)*

Those of you with exams next week – check the times and don't be late. The special farewell assembly starts in the main hall after lunch, I expect you all to attend. After that – you're on your own. Good luck. *Especially* you Jamie. You carry on like this and you're gonna need it.

(She pulls a cold, cold smile at **JAMIE**. **MISS HEDGE** *leaves – and the whole class turns on* **JAMIE***!)*

FATIMAH. Jamie! You have gotta tell us what happened! Oh my God!

JAMIE. I will do, but not here – I'll catch you outside, Pritti can get you started, she saw everything.

(The group descends on **PRITTI**, *who's basking in* **JAMIE**'*s reflected glory – her status in the group suddenly massively elevated, centre of attention!)*

PRITTI. Okay, so, first of all I was grounded, so I had to sort of jump out my bedroom window,

(She leads the class away, out of the room. **BEX** *and* **BECCA** *hang back, staring at* **JAMIE**, *whispering to each other. Then:)*

BECCA. Jamie –?

BEX. Jamie –?

JAMIE. Yeah, what?

BEX. Are you gonna go to prom in a dress?

JAMIE. No, of course not.

BECCA. *(Gasps!)* You are, aren't you!

JAMIE. A lady never tells.

(He gives them a smile and a wink.)

BEX & BECCA. This. Is. *Epic!*

(Giggling, they scurry away, leaving **JAMIE** *alone with a sullen* **DEAN**. **DEAN** *packs his bag and goes to leave.)*

JAMIE. Funny how things work out, in't it Dean?

*(***DEAN** *turns to him, goes to say something... then thinks better of it, turns to leave again.)*

Minger.

(Again – **DEAN** *turns, stares at* **JAMIE**.*)*

Minger, minger, minger, minger. Like that word could ever bring me down. Because I'm not a minger Dean. And you might be fit, and you might be handsome – but you're *so* ugly.

(**DEAN** *snarls – and suddenly strides towards* **JAMIE** *– superfast – dropping his bag – and in a second is right by* **JAMIE**, *his hands grabbing* **JAMIE***'s lapels – about to punch him!*)

(*...And* **JAMIE** *just leans up...*)

(*...And kisses* **DEAN**. *A playful peck – but* **DEAN** *takes a shocked step backwards – like it's him who's been punched!*)

(*Pause.* **DEAN** *staring daggers at* **JAMIE**, *working out how to play this.*)

DEAN. You think you're so special, don't you? You know, you're now't special, Jamie New.

JAMIE. Who's Jamie? I'm Mimi Me.

(*He exits.*)

DEAN. And she's now't special neither. Watch your back – *Mimi.*

(*He turns and strides away, boiling with fury.*)

[MUSIC NO. 09A 'SCENE CHANGE']

2. Jamie's House: Downstairs

(**MARGARET** *doing some housework, as* **RAY** *lets herself in.*)

RAY. Cooee! Only me!

MARGARET. Ey up!

RAY. Here, treat for you, got you your chocolate fix, three for one at the market.

(*She hands* **MARGARET** *some bars of chocolate.*)

MARGARET. A Murs Bar, a Kat-Kit and a Twox?

RAY. Three for one. Market. Beggars can't be. Where's Jamie? I got him a big bag of Maltoosers.

MARGARET. He's upstairs getting changed. You should have seen him leaving for school this morning – done up like Lana Turner. Cuppa?

RAY. Go on, I'm gasping. Ohhhh – I loved it at Legs Eleven, what a night – *what – a – night!*

MARGARET. I know – you were proper going for it.

RAY. I had to – they kept playing my song.

MARGARET. Which one's your song?

RAY. All of them! Hey, did I tell you – I met a new man.

MARGARET. Chuffing hell Ray – only you could pull in a drag club!

RAY. He's a doorman, called Norman.

MARGARET. What happened to that Dave?

RAY. Oh, I don't know Margaret, after a while the meat raffle just lost its allure. Still though – star of the show – our Jamie!

MARGARET. I know!

RAY. Star of the chuffing show! I mean, I knew he'd be good – but *wow!*

MARGARET. It's a lot to take on though, at his age, I mean you read about it don't you – child stars going off the rails.

RAY. Stop whittlin' woman, he's hardly Lindsay Lohan! Anyway, he's not a child, he's sixteen.

MARGARET. Sixteen's young.

RAY. Hey I was thinking, this weekend, girls day out, me and you, hit the shops at Meadow Hall, get you a new outfit.

MARGARET. I don't need a new outfit.

RAY. It's on me. Cos there's this speed-dating night, at the Black Bull, and I thought we could –

MARGARET. – No, I just want to focus on Jamie.

RAY. Oh, right. So he gets a new dress, he gets new shoes – and you get what exactly?

MARGARET. G'yaw Ray. Besides, he looks better in dresses than I do.

(Beat.)

Look, do you think, us encouraging him – have we done the right thing? I know he were amazing but –

(Bang bang bang at the sitting room door.)

JAMIE. *(Through door.)* Oi! Are you ready then?

RAY. For what love?

JAMIE. *(Through door.)* The big unveiling.

RAY. Of what?

> *(*JAMIE *bursts in through the sitting room door wearing his red dress – but it's now covered in fake fur, feathers, lace and sequins, massively OTT, with a big crazy fur/feather/ lace/sequin hat – an absolute showstopper!)*

JAMIE. The Limited Edition Prom Night Special!!!

> *(*MARGARET *and* RAY *look at him, lost for words.)*

MARGARET. ...*That's* your Prom Dress?!

JAMIE. It's the basic red number from Victor's Secret, but I made some *slight* amendments and accessorised accordingly. Do you like the fascinator?

RAY. Fascinator? Jamie love – that's a flippin' *Terminator*.

JAMIE. I know – I've been working really hard on this.

RAY. He has, bless him, look at that...craftsmanship.

JAMIE. I can't be seen wearing the same dress twice, I had to step it up a level.

MARGARET. Step it up a level?! This is...you've gone too far – this is too much.

JAMIE. Too much? No, I think it's actually quite subtle. Look –

> *(He manipulates a concealed switch and the dress lights up – it's covered in integrated Christmas tree lights.)*

RAY. Chuffin' hell!

JAMIE. No, hang on.

> *(He presses the control again, and the lights start flashing in sequence.)*

RAY. Oh my God –

[MUSIC NO. 10 'LIMITED EDITION']

There is *nothing* about this that I do not love!

LIMITED EDITION PROM NIGHT SPECIAL
TAKE IT FROM ME TOO MUCH IS NEVER TOO MUCH
LIMITED EDITION PROM NIGHT SPECIAL
BETTER TAKE A PICTURE COS IT'S LOOK AND DON'T
    TOUCH

LIMITED EDITION, CORONATION
LADIES GIVE A CURTSEY COS HERE COMES YOUR QUEEN
LIMITED EDITION, CELEBRATION
PRESTIGIOUS AND PRODIGIOUS AND HE'S ONLY SIXTEEN!

RAY.	JAMIE.	ENSEMBLE.
WHO'S GOT		WHO?
THE HEAT?	WHO?	WHO?
WHO'S GOT		WHO?
THE HEELS?	WHO?	WHO?
WHO'S GOT		WHO?
THE PERKS?		WHO?
	YEAH – THIRTY-	WHO?
	SIX D!	A-WHO?
WHO'S GOT	ME!	A-WHO?
THE CLASS?		WHO?
WHO'S GOT	ME!	WHO?
THE ASS?		WHO?
WHO'S GOT		WHO?
THE WORKS!		WHO?
	MIMI ME!!!	MIMI ME!!!

JAMIE.

LIMITED EDITION, SO ENCHANTING
SERVING LITTY REALNESS AND I'M FRESHER THAN FRESH

RAY.

LIMITED EDITION, DEBUTANTING
WORSHIPPING THE BODICE OF A GODDESS MADE FLESH!

JAMIE & RAY.	ENSEMBLE.
TURNING THE IGNITION!	
	TURNING THE IGNITION!
TAKING POLE POSITION	
	TAKING POLE POSITION
MIMI'S ON A MISSION!	
	MIMI'S ON A MISSION
KILL THE COMPETITION!	
	KILL THE COMPETITION!
HERE'S THE	
AMMUNITION!	
	HERE'S THE
	AMMUNITION!
LIMITED EDITION	
PROM NIGHT SPECIAL!	PROM NIGHT SPECIAL!

MARGARET.	ENSEMBLE
WHAT HAVE I DONE?	
	DONE
LETTING HIM RUN?	
	RUN
GOING SO FAST	
	FAST
HOW LONG CAN IT LAST?	

JAMIE.	RAY & ENSEMBLE.
	LIMITED EDITION
CELEBRATION! WOMEN MAY BE BORN BUT DIVAS ARE MADE	
	LIMITED EDITION
GRADUATION I KNOW WHERE I'M GOING DON'T BE THROWING NO SHADE	

JAMIE & RAY.	ENSEMBLE.
LIMITED EDITION	LIMITED EDITION
PROM NIGHT SPECIAL	
TAKE IT FROM ME	
TOO MUCH IS NEVER TOO MUCH	
LIMITED EDITION	LIMITED EDITION
PROM NIGHT SPECIAL	

JAMIE.
   BETTER TAKE A PICTURE COS IT'S LOOK AT ME
RAY.
   LOOK AT HIM
JAMIE.
   LOOK AT ME
RAY.
   LOOK AT HIM
JAMIE.
   LOOK AT ME

RAY.

   LOOK AT HIM!

JAMIE.

   LOOK AND DON'T –

   (The phone rings, cutting off the end of **JAMIE***'s song.* **JAMIE** *looks annoyed, then answers the phone.)*

Hello!

   (Something is said at the other end.)

Oh, yeah, okay, okay, yeah. Mum, it's the school.

   [MUSIC NO. 10A 'SCENE CHANGE']

3. Mayfield School: Miss Hedge's Office

(MISS HEDGE, alone in her office, sitting on her desk in her stocking feet, her precious Jimmy Choos on the floor beneath her. She's on her mobile, leaving an awkward voicemail.)

MISS HEDGE. Hi Paul, it's Janet calling, again, I was just ringing to say how much I enjoyed our dinner last week, I actually left you a message already but I guess you didn't – well anyway, I'd love to do it again, that would be...cool.

(Winces at her choice of words – 'cool'?!)

So, um, call me – or if you don't get the time...I'll call you. So – I'll talk to you later, bye Paul, bye, bye, bye.

(She hangs up, unsure of how that went. Deep breath. Armour on. She's bulletproof again. Her desk phone rings, she answers:)

Yes? Yes, send them in please.

(She sits on her desk chair, slips on her Jimmy Choos, and the armour is complete.)

(MARGARET, RAY and JAMIE enter.)

Come in, sit down.

MARGARET. So what's this about?

MISS HEDGE. I'm sorry to call you in like this Mrs New, but as I said, there's been a complaint.

MARGARET. What do you mean – a complaint?

MISS HEDGE. Jamie. *Jamie.* There's rumours going around that you plan to attend School Prom in a dress. Is this true?

JAMIE. Yes. It is.

MISS HEDGE. Jamie – the school prom is an event for everyone – it's something the entire school has been looking forward to. It's not fair for you to hijack it.

JAMIE. I won't be!

MISS HEDGE. Jamie, the *other* students –

JAMIE. – They won't mind! They love it!

MISS HEDGE. Well that's where you're wrong love. As I said, there's been complaints.

MARGARET. I'm sorry – what sort of complaints?

MISS HEDGE. I've had a very angry, confused and disturbed parent on the phone this afternoon, demanding to know if it were true that we, Mayfield School, were turning his son's prom into a freakshow.

JAMIE. I'm not a freak!

MISS HEDGE. The word he used – the exact word he used –

(She pauses, before delivering the fatal blow:)

– was *disgusting*.

JAMIE. Disgusting? I'm not disgusting...

MISS HEDGE. Not my word, as I'm sure you can appreciate, and I did not want it to come to this, but Jamie – I *warned* you. Because of what *you've* done – the matter has been taken out of my hands. I can't just ignore the feelings of the other parents.

RAY. Ignore the feelings of a *bigot*!

MISS HEDGE. I don't think language like that is very helpful, do you Mrs, uh – I'm sorry, I'm not quite sure why you're here.

RAY. I'm family. As good as.

MISS HEDGE. Well that's certainly unconventional. And I can see where Jamie gets it from, but Jamie, let me be very clear: Mimi Me is not a student at this school. Jamie New is. And if you want to come to Prom, you come as Jamie. In a jacket, and a shirt and a pair of trousers, just like every other boy. I'm sorry, but that's just the way it is.

MARGARET. No, that's not good enough.

MISS HEDGE. My hands are tied Mrs New. Maybe *you* shouldn't have encouraged him.

MARGARET. Come on Jamie. We've heard enough.

RAY. I don't know how you sleep at night. Shame on you.

> (MARGARET *shakes her head, leads* RAY *and* JAMIE *out of the office, into the corridor.*)

> (JAMIE *keeps walking ahead – when he meets* DEAN, *heading towards him with a big grin on his face, like he knows exactly what's just happened.*)

DEAN. Eh, some people's parents can be so intolerant, can't they *Mimi*?

> (JAMIE *runs offstage, hiding his shame.*)

[MUSIC NO. 10B 'SCENE CHANGE']

4. Pritti's Bedroom

(Pritti's room is tidy, ordered and full of books. Instead of pin-ups of boys, she has maps of the world and historical figures. **PRITTI** *sits on her bed as* **JAMIE** *paces the room.)*

JAMIE. 'Disgusting'! How could she call Mimi Me 'disgusting'?! Mimi is gorgeous, and glamorous – and look at Miss Hedge in her knock-off Jimmy Choos – she's just jealous, she is! She *wishes* she was Mimi Me!

PRITTI. Jamie! Calm down! My mum and dad'll hear you – I'm not meant to have boys in my room.

JAMIE. Oh I'm sorry, please hold me back whilst I try not to ravish you.

PRITTI. Jamie! House rules! Come on!

*(***JAMIE*** sighs, then sits on the bed next to her. Pause.)*

JAMIE. Your room's so tidy, I don't know how you do it.

PRITTI. I don't have as many dresses as you do.

JAMIE. I like your lamp.

PRITTI. Thanks.

(Pause.)

Jamie, do you think... Miss Hedge maybe has a point? You are a bit...you know...of a...drama queen.

JAMIE. I am so *not* a drama queen!!!

*(***PRITTI*** raises an eyebrow.)*

...Fine.

PRITTI. I'm not saying I'm on her side, but she is right about one thing – prom in't just about you.

JAMIE. I wasn't making it about me!

PRITTI. Jamie – your dress is self-illuminating!

JAMIE. No! That's *Mimi Me*! That's how she dresses!

PRITTI. Why does Mimi Me have to be part of the equation?! I'm gonna be a doctor – it doesn't mean I have to go everywhere swinging my stethoscope. Why not just wear something simple to prom? Something modest. Not a drag queen, but a really beautiful boy.

JAMIE. There's nothing beautiful about me.

PRITTI. Jamie...you are *stunning*.

> *(Beat.)*

You know, you've never asked me why I wear a hijab.

JAMIE. I know why – cos of your dad.

PRITTI. No! You see Jamie – sometimes you forget that other people...we're not all just your backing singers. You've never asked me – so go on, ask.

JAMIE. Why do you wear a hijab?

PRITTI. Because I want to. Because it keeps me simple. Because it frames who I am.

JAMIE. Are you saying...I should wear a burka?

PRITTI. No! I'm saying...don't go there to put on a show. Just go there as *you*.

JAMIE. But without *her*...I'm just ugly.

> *(Pause.)*

PRITTI. You know there's a name like Jamie in Arabic: Jamil. So if you were Pakistani or Middle Eastern or whatever, they'd call you Jamil New –

[MUSIC NO. 11 'IT MEANS BEAUTIFUL']

And do you know what Jamil means? It means beautiful.

IT MEANS SOMETHING THAT'S ONLY YOURS TO GIVE
IT MEANS CHOOSING THE WAY YOU WANT TO LIVE
IT MEANS WONDERFUL
AND IT MEANS POWERFUL
AND IT MEANS TRUE.
IT MEANS SOMETHING AS PERFECT AS IT'S PURE
IT MEANS WAITING UNTIL YOU KNOW YOU'RE SURE
IT MEANS BEAUTIFUL

AND IT'S BEAUTIFUL
LIKE YOU.

BEAUTIFUL
BEAUTIFUL
A LITTLE BIT OF GLITTER IN THE GREY
BEAUTIFUL
BEAUTIFUL
SOMETHING PRECIOUS YOU DON'T SIMPLY GIVE AWAY

IT MEANS SOMETHING THAT'S ALWAYS YOURS TO KEEP
IT'S THE FACE YOU DON'T TAKE OFF TO GO TO SLEEP
IT MEANS SIMPLE
AND IT MEANS MAGICAL
LIKE A KISS.
IT'S A PATH THAT YOU CHOOSE TO WALK UPON
NOT SOME FLEETING THING YOU FIND ONE DAY IS GONE
IT MEANS INNOCENCE
IT MEANS CONFIDENCE
LIKE THIS.

BEAUTIFUL
BEAUTIFUL
A LITTLE BIT OF GLITTER IN THE GREY
BEAUTIFUL
BEAUTIFUL
SOMETHING PRECIOUS YOU DON'T RUSH TO GIVE AWAY

BEAUTIFUL.

JAMIE. One day, when I were eight, me dad come home early from work, and he caught me dressing up. It were this old thing of me mum's, sierra gold, this maxi dress, it was way too long for me so I'd sort of tied it in a knot at the side and I was swishing it about and lip-syncing along to Patsy Cline, like you do, and there he was, you know, just stood in the doorway, just staring at me...the look on his face...and he said...well *what* he said has made me feel ugly me entire life.

PRITTI. But he sent you the card and the flowers to your show. He paid for your dress. I mean it's strange in't it? Don't you think Jamie? It's strange.

(She has an inkling of the truth.)

JAMIE. I guess.

PRITTI. I think you should go and talk to him.

JAMIE. Yeah, maybe.

PRITTI. You could go now. Not that I'm trying to get rid of you or 'owt.

*(**JAMIE** goes to leave, then pauses.)*

JAMIE. If I don't say it enough – you are the best friend a boy who sometimes wants to be a girl could ever ask for.

*(He kisses **PRITTI** on the cheek, then leaves.)*

*(**PRITTI** touches her cheek where he kissed her.)*

[MUSIC NO. 11A 'IT MEANS BEAUTIFUL (REPRISE)']

PRITTI.

IT'S A SECRET YOU NEVER GET TO TELL
SOMETHING SHY AND SPECIAL STUCK INSIDE ITS SHELL
IT MEANS BRILLIANT
AND RESILIENT
BUT NOT FREE.

BEAUTIFUL
BEAUTIFUL
IS A PROMISE THAT'S STILL WAITING FOR ITS DAY
BEAUTIFUL
BEAUTIFUL
IT'S A LEADING PART I'LL MAYBE GET TO PLAY
BEAUTIFUL

5. Jamie's Dad's House

(A house that's a lot smarter than Jamie's house, but nothing too grand. **JAMIE** *nervously approaches. He takes a few deep breaths, and finds the courage to knock.)*

(After a moment, **JAMIE'S DAD** *opens the door.)*

JAMIE'S DAD. Jamie?!

JAMIE. Hiya Dad. You alright?

> *(***JAMIE***'s nervous, but determined not to show it.)*

JAMIE'S DAD. You can't come in, we've got friends 'round.

JAMIE. This'll only take a moment. I just wanted to say thank you for the flowers and the dress.

JAMIE'S DAD. What flowers? What dress?

JAMIE. At me show. You sent me flowers. The card said –

JAMIE'S DAD. What show?

JAMIE. At me drag show. At Legs Eleven. I were on stage. My debut.

JAMIE'S DAD. Your what?

JAMIE. I thought you knew – Mum said –

JAMIE'S DAD. – You got up on a *stage*?!

JAMIE. They all loved her Dad!

JAMIE'S DAD. Her? Her who?

> *(And now* **JAMIE** *feels so naked, exposed, foolish – saying the name –)*

JAMIE. Mimi Me.

JAMIE'S DAD. Mimi Me. What sort of a name is that?

JAMIE. It's funny!

JAMIE'S DAD. It's *funny*? You dressed up, in public –

JAMIE. You paid for me dress! You sent me flowers!

JAMIE'S DAD. I sent you *n'owt*!

> *(***JAMIE** *absorbs this thunderbolt.)*

Aren't you ashamed of your'sen?

(**JAMIE** *looks up at his dad, answers with great courage:*)

JAMIE. No.

JAMIE'S DAD. Well you *should* be. I wanted a son so badly. And I got you.

(*He slams the door in* **JAMIE**'s *face.*)

[MUSIC NO. 12 'UGLY IN THIS UGLY WORLD']

JAMIE.

THERE'S A PLACE WHERE I BELONG
THERE'S A PLACE WHERE I BELONG
FOR THE KID WHO CAME OUT WRONG
THERE'S A PLACE WHERE I BELONG

FAR FROM YOUR FATHER'S EYES
LOST IN YOUR MOTHER'S LIES
UGLY IN THIS UGLY WORLD IS ALL I AM

TENORS & BARITONES.

YEEAAAOW!

JAMIE.

WHY AM I EVEN HERE?
CAN'T I JUST DISAPPEAR?

JAMIE.	**TENORS & BARITONES.**
UGLY IS THE ONLY THING THAT'S TRUE NOW	AH
UGLY POISONS EV'RYTHING I DO NOW	AH
AND FILTH AND SHAME AND UGLINESS IS WHO I AM	AH
I AM!	
OOH UGLY IS AN UGLY FACE AND	AH
UGLY IS AN UGLY KID	
UGLY IS THIS UGLY PLACE WHERE	AH
UGLY DOES WHAT UGLY DID	
UGLY IN THIS UGLY WORLD IS ALL I AM	UGLY IN THIS UGLY WORLD IS ALL I AM
ALL I AM...	

6. Jamie's House

(**MARGARET** *sitting at the kitchen table, needle and thread out, making repairs to the red dress to distract herself from how worried she is.* **JAMIE** *enters – slow, distant, all the sparkle gone from him.*)

(*He just stares, frozen. Then he points to the red dress.*)

JAMIE. Who bought me that?

MARGARET. Where've you been?

JAMIE. Who bought me that?

MARGARET. Well you saw – it said on't card –

JAMIE. I've been to his house.

> (*Pause.* **MARGARET** *can't hold his eye. Then* **JAMIE** *realises:*)

Where's your necklace Mum? Where's your gold necklace?

MARGARET. ...I sold it.

> (**JAMIE** *points to the dress.*)

JAMIE. For that?

> (*Pause. Then* **MARGARET** *nods.*)

What else was from you? The flowers?

> (**MARGARET** *nods.*)

The birthday card? How many birthday cards? How many years? Me whole life??

MARGARET. Jamie –

JAMIE. How could you lie to me, Mum?

MARGARET. I just wanted you to be happy.

JAMIE. So you lied!

MARGARET. ...Yeah.

JAMIE. Yeah?

> (*He strides over to a drawer, pulls out a pair of scissors – goes to attack the dress with them.*)

MARGARET. No!

JAMIE. Right, give it me.

MARGARET. What are you doing?

JAMIE. I don't want it now!

MARGARET. Jamie – don't spoil that dress!

> *(She snatches the dress off* **JAMIE** *– he tries to pull it back away from her.)*

JAMIE. I said GIVE –

> *(Rrrrrrrrrip! The dress rips.)*

You ruin *everything*. Stop living your life through me! Just cos you've never been *anyone*! No wonder Dad left you!

> *(He runs out the front door, leaving* **MARGARET** *alone.)*

> *(And there she is, clutching a ripped, ruined red dress.)*

[MUSIC NO. 13 'HE'S MY BOY']

MARGARET.
> THE COLD EMPTY MORNINGS,
> THE COFFEE CUP WARNINGS,
> REMEMB'RING THE SPARK
> THAT LIVED IN A LOVE
> THAT DIED IN THE DARK
> BUT LIFE KEEPS YOU GUESSING.
> ALONG CAME A BLESSING.
> MY WORLD WAS AWAKE
> MY PRECIOUS SURPRISE
> MY PERFECT MISTAKE
>
> AND MAYBE HE'LL BREAK MY HEART
> COS HE'LL TAKE MY HEART
> WHEN HE GOES,
> I'M DREADING THE DAY WHEN HE JUST WALKS AWAY
>
> HE'S MY BOY
> HE DRIVES ME INSANE,

HE'S MY BOY.
MY PLEASURE, MY PAIN,
HE'S MY BOY.
BELIEVE ME, HE DON'T MAKE IT EASY,
HE'LL OWN ME UNTIL
HE'S OUTGROWN ME, BUT STILL, HE'S MY BOY
HE'S MY BOY.

FROM THE MOMENT I SAW HIM,
NO MAN CAME BEFORE HIM
HE TAUGHT ME TO FIGHT,
TO KNOCK BACK THE BLACK,
TO LET IN THE LIGHT

AND MAYBE HE'LL BREAK MY HEART
COS HE'LL TAKE MY HEART
WHEN HE GOES,
IT'S CRUEL THAT HE CAN, BUT THAT'S JUST LIKE A MAN,

HE'S MY BOY.
MY BLESSING, MY CURSE
HE'S MY BOY.
FOR BETTER, FOR WORSE
HE'S MY BOY.
BELIEVE ME, HE DON'T MAKE IT EASY.
HE NEEDS ME, FULFILLS ME
THEN BLEEDS ME BUT STILL, HE'S MY BOY.
HE'S MY BOY.

AND DON'T TELL ME I'M FOOLING MYSELF, FALLING
    AGAIN
COS I KNOW THE PATTERN, I KNOW THE PRICE, AND I
    KNOW THE MEN
AND I KNOW THE BRIGHT LIGHTS ARE GOING TO TEMPT
    HIM TO STRAY
BUT I'D TRADE MY TOMORROWS – TO HAVE HIM TODAY!
TODAY!
TODAY!
HE'S MY –
HE'S MY –
HE'S MY –

MARGARET.
> HE'S MY BOY
> AND BOYS ALWAYS GROW,
> HE'S MY BOY.
> AND BOYS ALWAYS GO,
> HE'S MY BOY.
> HE'S BLINDED AND SO BLOODY MINDED,
> HE'S CLUELESS AND CLEVER,
> CONFUSING BUT EVER MY BOY!
>
> HE'S MY VOICE,
> HE'S MY CHANCE,
> HE'S MY SMILE,
> HE'S MY DAY,
> HE'S MY LIFE,
> HE'S MY PAIN,
> HE'S MY JOY.
>
> HE'S MY BABY,
> HE'S MY MAN.
> HE'S MY BOY.

7. Bus Station

[MUSIC NO. 14 'AND YOU DON'T EVEN KNOW IT (BUS STATION REPRISE)']

(A cold, unlovely bus station in the centre of town. **JAMIE** *staggers into view, swaying as if drunk.)*

JAMIE.

THERE'S A CLOCK ON THE WALL AND IT'S MOVING TOO
SLOW
BUT MIMI ME'S GOT PLACES TO GO
AND SHE'S WAITED TOO LONG AND HER WAITING IS DONE
NOW SHE'S FINDING HER FEET AND SHE'S READY TO RUN

YEAH, I'M A – SUPERSTAR – AND YOU DON'T EVEN KNOW IT
IN A – WONDERBRA – AND YOU DON'T EVEN KNOW IT
YOU'RE SO – BLAH BLAH – AND YOU DON'T EVEN KNOW IT
AND THAT'S – ALL YOU ARE – AND YOU DON'T EVEN KNOW
IT

(A **GANG OF LADS** *enter, hoods up, anonymous, and start circling 'round* **JAMIE.** *Blind to the danger,* **JAMIE** *starts to vamp as Mimi Me, dancing for them.)*

AND I'M COMING UP
IN A DOUBLE-D CUP
COS WHEN A BOY'S THIS STACKED
HE'S THE HEADLINE ACT

YOU LITTLE PEOPLE IN MY WAY
KEEP GETTING SMALLER EV'RY DAY
I'M BURSTING AT THE SEAMS!
AND I'M GONNA BE THE ONE!
GET OFF MY STAGE, GET IN YOUR PLACE
SIT BACK AND MEMORISE THIS FACE
YOU'LL SEE IT IN YOUR DREAMS
AND I'M GONNA KISS THE –

LAD 1.

FILTHY LITTLE –

LAD 2.
> DIRTY LITTLE –

LAD 3.
> UGLY LITTLE –

LAD 1, LAD 2 & LAD 3.
> QUEER!

>> *(The **LADS** attack **JAMIE,** punching him to the ground, swift and vicious. One of them spits on him as he falls. Then:)*

HUGO. Oi! Leave him alone!

>> *(He runs over – and the **LADS** scarper.)*

You little thugs!

>> *(Painfully, **JAMIE** pulls himself up onto the bus-stop bench. He's so broken now, and so lost.)*

Jamie? Oh Jamie love!

>> *(He cradles **JAMIE** gently.)*

Let me see your face – oh, I'll ruddy kill 'em!!!

JAMIE. Hugo, what are *you* doing here?

HUGO. What, you think I sleep in the shop? What are you doing here.

JAMIE. I'm running away. But I don't think I'm very good at it. I were going to London. Where the streets are paved with gold and lit by dreams.

HUGO. What have *you* got to run away from?

JAMIE. Everything! Me life's a mess! I'm nobody! I'm nothing! I'm disgusting and nothing and vile and *nothing*!

HUGO. Jamie! Never say such terrible things!

JAMIE. Well that's what *he* thinks!

HUGO. Who?

JAMIE. ...Me dad.

HUGO. He said that did he? Oh Jamie, don't listen to him. He's a silly ignorant man, that's all.

JAMIE. Then how come I feel, so hard, in here...

> *(Hits his gut.)*

...that he's right?

> *(Pause.)*

What's me story Hugo? What's The Legend Of Jamie New?

HUGO. Once upon a time there were a boy who did everything ten times faster and ten times louder than everyone else, and he were fearless, and terrified, and a genius, and an idiot, and a star...and a failure. I think I'm talking more about me now.

JAMIE. You're not a failure, though. You're Loco Chanelle.

HUGO. The Legend Of Loco Chanelle – you know how that ends? With me, sitting here, with you, at this bus stop.

JAMIE. And everything else along the way! Your story's amazing.

HUGO. But it's just a story Jamie. It's not true. Oh, John were real enough. And I loved him. And it broke me. And Loco...she made some shocking choices, that one.

> *(Pause.)*

I look at you, and this world, and how you live in it, and how everything's changing so fast, and I think...what do I know anymore? I'm so bloody old, I'm out of date, and you're just... New.

JAMIE. What does that mean? I don't know who I am!

HUGO. You're sixteen! Of course you don't, you're still cooking! Oh Jamie – you've got *everything* to look forward to! *This* is your story – and it's happening right now.

JAMIE. And what happens next? How does it end Hugo?

HUGO. I don't know Jamie. It's for you to write that.

> *(**JAMIE** wipes his eyes – and runs offstage.)*

[MUSIC NO. 14A 'OVER THE TOP (REPRISE)']

8. Jamie's House

(**JAMIE** *walks home, head low – to find* **RAY** *sitting on the wall outside, waiting.*)

RAY. Ah, the wanderer returns. She's inside, waiting.

(**JAMIE** *stares at her, ashamed, lost for words.*)

Seems to me like everyone's been giving you advice recently.

(*Beat.*)

Well you'll get none of that from me. You've always known who you are Jamie New, better than most of us, and maybe you'd have been just fine all along if it weren't for everyone else interfering, always telling you what's best for you. Well right now you've got a job to do, so get on in there and step up. Right, well, I've said my piece.

(*She stands and goes to leave.*)

JAMIE. Ray...

(*She turns back to him.*)

...I don't think I've got a dad anymore.

RAY. I'm sorry cookie. That's rough. But you've always got me.

(*She walks away.* **JAMIE** *takes a deep breath and heads inside.*)

[MUSIC NO. 14B 'SCENE CHANGE']

9. Jamie's House

(**JAMIE** *enters. The room is dark.* **MARGARET** *sits on the sofa, staring into space.*)

JAMIE. I'm sorry Mum.

(**MARGARET** *looks 'round – sees his black eye.*)

MARGARET. Jamie – your face!

JAMIE. I'm fine, I'm fine. Just…a stupid thing that I did. That I won't be doing again.

MARGARET. Sit down.

(*She gets the first-aid kit and starts to clean* **JAMIE***'s wound.*)

I'm sorry I lied.

JAMIE. Why did you do it Mum?

MARGARET. I were just trying to protect you.

JAMIE. But you must have known, in the end, I'd find out.

MARGARET. I didn't think it through did I?

(**JAMIE** *winces as she touches his eye.*)

Sorry.

JAMIE. It's alright. I deserve it.

MARGARET. No Jamie. You don't deserve any of this.

(*Pause.*)

The only man I ever loved was your dad. Choosing a man like that…

(*Beat.*)

He were never good for either of us. I can see that now.

JAMIE. Well, who needs a dad anyway? I've got Ray. She's twice the man he'll ever be. And with bigger balls.

MARGARET. I know you're not going to be around forever –

JAMIE. Mum, I'm sixteen, you've still got me for a couple more years. I'll still be putting out bins on a Monday morning. I'll just be doing it in a pair of heels.

(*Pause.*)

Mum…do you ever wish I were just normal?

MARGARET. No! Never! And anyway, what is normal – this *is* normal for you!

JAMIE. If I were normal I could go to prom. If I were normal Dad would've stayed.

MARGARET. Your dad's an idiot. You've done n'owt wrong Jamie – you never did. But I am sorry. I'm sorry for him. Because he's missing out on *so much*. I mean, look at you. And you can still go to prom.

[MUSIC NO. 15 'MY MAN, YOUR BOY']

And I don't care if you go in trousers or a dress or wearing nothing at all – as long as you go as *you*. Because whatever you do – you are always *beautiful*.

JAMIE.

BEAUTY IS THE FACE I SEE
SMILIN' RIGHT IN FRONT OF ME
I'VE BEEN SO DUMB
COS YOU ARE BEAUTIFUL, MY MUM

ME BIRTHDAY SHOES WERE MEANT TO ROAM
BUT BEAUTY'S IN THE COMING HOME
AND FEELING FREE
YOU ARE MORE BEAUTIFUL THAN ME

AND I HAVE SEEN A LIGHT THAT'S SHINING BRIGHT AND
    IT'S BEEN BRIGHTER THAN I KNEW,
AND IT'S A LIGHT THAT PASSED ME BY BUT IT SHINES
    RIGHT FROM YOU, MY MUM!

I'M SORRY FOR THE STUPID THINGS I'VE DONE
I'M SORRY FOR THE STRANGER I'VE BECOME
AND I'D BE NOTHING IF YOU'D NOT BEEN THERE,
TO CARE

AND NOW!

MARGARET.

I'D GIVE MY LIFE TO SEE YOU SMILE

JAMIE.

I'LL GET OUT THERE AND SHOW THE WORLD – AND HOW!

MARGARET.

I THOUGHT I'D LOST YOU FOR A WHILE

JAMIE.

COS YOU AND ME AIN'T EASY TO DESTROY

MARGARET.

AND I WILL ALWAYS BE YOUR BIGGEST FAN

MY MAN

JAMIE.

YOUR BOY

MARGARET. Give us a love.

(**JAMIE** *hugs her – holding her so tight.*)

10. Mayfield School Exterior

[MUSIC NO. 16 'THE PROM SONG']

*(The outside of the school. The **BOYS** emerge in their hired tuxedos, full of the joys.)*

BOYS (DEAN, CY, LEVI, SAYID & MICKEY).

ALL THE BOYS AT THE PROM ARE LOOKING PRETTY FLY
SAY OH OH OH OH OH
ALL THE GIRLS AT THE PROM ARE LOOKING FOR A GUY
SAY OH

CY.

SEE THAT GIRL – I'M SCOPING THE BLONDE

MICKEY.

CAST MY SPELL – I'M WAVING MY WAND

DEAN.

CHECK YOUR SUIT OUT – MAN YOU WERE CONNED

SAYID.

CHECK THIS CUMMERBUND – MAN I'M JAMES BOND!

*(The **GIRLS** all run in, even more excitable, dolled up in their new gowns.)*

BECCA & BEX.

NO SHE DIDN'T!
WHAT IS SHE WEARING?!
NO SHE DIDN'T!
I *LOVE* WHAT YOU'RE WEARING

FATIMAH & VICKY.

LADIES IN THE CLASS
LADIES IN THE CLASS
CHECK US FROM THE BACK:
PIPPA MIDDLETON'S ASS

GIRLS (FATIMAH, VICKY, BEX & BECCA).

WE'RE PRETTY IN OUR DRESSES
PRETTY AS PRINCESSES
STRUTTIN' WITH MY SISTERS
THE SHOES ARE WORTH THE BLISTERS

ALL.

I'VE GOT A DREAM!

GIRLS.

I'VE GOT A DRESS!

BOYS.

I'VE TIED A BOWTIE TO IMPRESS!

ALL.

TODAY'S MY LUCKY DAY
AND I'M GONNA BE THE ONE!
AND IF OUR FUTURE AIN'T SO BRIGHT
WE'LL STILL BE SHINING FOR ONE NIGHT!
TOMORROW'S YEARS AWAY
AND WE'RE GONNA KISS THE SUN!

SAYID.

I'M GONNA HAVE SOME FUN!

BEX, VICKI, DEAN, CY, SAYID & MICKEY.

OH, OH, OH!

BECCA.	**BEX, VICKI, DEAN, CY, SAYID & MICKEY.**
BE THE ONE	OH, OH, OH!
FATIMAH.	
I'M GONNA KISS	OH, OH, OH!
THE SUN	
BECCA.	
COS I'M GONNA	OH, OH, OH!
BE THE ONE	
	OH, OH, OH!
FATIMAH & BECCA.	
I'M GONNA KISS	OH, OH, OH!
THE SUN!	
FATIMAH.	
BE THE ONE!	OH, OH, OH!

BEX & BECCA. Bloody hell Pritti!

> (*The music cuts out as the* **GIRLS** *part – and
> we see* **PRITTI,** *in her prom dress, looking
> nervous and a bit uncomfortable, making her
> way across the car park. She's still wearing
> her hijab – but it's in a beautiful blue, to*

*match the elegant and modest blue dress
she's wearing. Her arms are covered and she's
dressed very modestly – but she is wearing
makeup. Not very much – but for* **PRITTI** *it's
a big step.)*

BEX. Look at you – wearing makeup!

*(***PRITTI*** isn't sure if this a compliment or a
criticism.)*

PRITTI. ...Yeah?

BEX. Looks really nice on you.

PRITTI. *(Phew!)* Thanks.

BECCA. Love your dress Pritti. Looks lush on you.

PRITTI. Thanks Becca. I like yours too.

BECCA. Thanks. I had it made special. That blue suits you.
I mean it's not what I'd have worn but – it suits you.

PRITTI. I don't think I'd have worn your dress either Becca –
but it suits you too.

*(And for the first time there's a bit of an edge
to* **PRITTI***'s voice – like she's standing up for
herself a bit and giving as good as she gets.)*

*(***FATIMAH*** enters, dressed also in a blue hijab
and modest dress, basically wearing the same
outfit as* **PRITTI***. She sees* **PRITTI***. Stops. Stares.)*

FATIMAH. Oh bloody hell! MUM!!! I need a new hijab!

(She rushes back offstage.)

*(***SAYID, MICKEY, CY*** and **LEVI** saunter over.)*

CY. Hey! Looking fine ladies!

VICKI. Boys in suits – get them! Think you're all James Bond.

LEVI. License To Thrill innit, cos I'm gonna thrill you with
my –

BECCA & BEX. *– Shut up Levi.*

VICKI. I have to say though Sayid – you do scrub up well.

SAYID. Hey, I *always* dress the part. I only ever wear designer clothes you know – Nike, Puma, Adidas, you get me?

> (*It's such a lovely mood – all laughter and banter.* **PRITTI** *plucks up the courage to join in.*)

PRITTI. I think it's great everyone's made such an effort.

> (**DEAN** *appears, looking very smart in his tux.*)

DEAN. And who asked you? Oh my God – look at makeup on it. I thought there were only one drag queen at this school. Must be contagious.

> (**PRITTI** *is instantly cowed.*)

BEX. Shut up Dean.

DEAN. Oh sorry – my mistake – it's Krusty The Klown, innit. Hiya Krusty. Is Homer and Marge here with you too? Did you all ride in together in your little clown car?

BECCA. Shut up Dean! Why do you have to be such a moron!

DEAN. And why does she have to be such a waccy spaccy virgin?

BECCA. Dean!

PRITTI. It's alright. It doesn't matter.

DEAN. What did it say?

> (**PRITTI** *looks up – and stares* **DEAN** *full in the face for the first time.*)

PRITTI. I said – it doesn't matter. And that's the truth Dean. What you say, what you think, what you do…it doesn't matter anymore. No, I am not a 'spac' – as you so ignorantly call it. What I am – is clever. Cleverer than you. But if you want to turn that into an insult that's fine – knock yourself out. Because tomorrow we're done. Exams are over, school's finished. And I start getting on with the rest of my life. But *you* – tomorrow…you're nothing. This school is your world.

PRITTI. No more big fish, no more small pond. You've got –

> *(Checks watch.)*

– five hours left of being someone who anyone actually cares about, and that's it. *Five hours.* So call me spaccy if it makes you happy, but enjoy it while you can, because your time's almost up.

> *(She goes to leave – then stops, not finished yet.)*

And yeah I am a virgin, and I'm proud of that too.

> *(Pause.)*

SAYID. Whoa man, she *totally* nailed you!

> *(**PRITTI** moves away. **DEAN**, furious, tries to get a parting insult in.)*

DEAN. Yeah well – you, you – couldn't even get a date to the prom!

> *(**PRITTI** stops – turns back to him.)*

PRITTI. What are you talking about? I'm here with him.

> *(And everyone turns to see **JAMIE** in a dress – not Mimi, but **JAMIE** – simple, white, elegant, chic, minimal makeup, no wig.)*

> *(A cry goes up from the crowd – 'Jamie! Jamie! Oh my God!' **JAMIE** just stands there, being the bravest he's ever been.)*

> *(**DEAN** walks off in disgust.)*

> *(**BEX** and **BECCA** go up to him, the first to break the spell.)*

BEX & BECCA. *Jamie...*

> *(**JAMIE** isn't sure if they're horrified or impressed.)*

JAMIE. ...Yeah?

BEX. You look...

JAMIE. ...Yeah?

> *(Beat.)*

BEX & BECCA. *Iconic!*

JAMIE. Oh thanks!

BEX & BECCA. *Can we have a selfie?*

JAMIE. Yeah! Course you can!

> *(And suddenly all the kids are running over to him, pulling out phones, asking for photos.)*

SAYID. Eh – if I didn't know I *totally* would!

> *(**BEX** and **BECCA** cluster 'round **JAMIE** as they take their selfies. **JAMIE** hugs **PRITTI** into the picture.)*

BEX. Over here Becca, help me pick a filter.

> *(**BECCA** and **BEX** move off.)*

> *(**PRITTI** goes up to **JAMIE**, hugs him.)*

PRITTI. You made it.

JAMIE. Course I did. You look beautiful.

PRITTI. So do you.

RAY. *(Offstage.)* Hold back – you'll embarrass him!

MARGARET. *(Offstage.)* It's just one photo!

RAY. *(Offstage.)* You've already got a thousand!

MARGARET. *(Offstage.)* Then it's a thousand and one!

JAMIE. Mum, Ray, it's fine – we can see you.

> *(**RAY** and **MARGARET** sheepishly enter from the side of the stage.)*

MARGARET. Sorry love – we didn't want to embarrass you.

RAY. We were just checking up on you cookie, making sure you don't tuck your dress in your knickers or now't. *Oh kiddah* Pritti? *Masha Allah*, you look gorgeous love.

PRITTI. Thanks *Auntie-ji*, you alright Margaret.

MARGARET. Hiya love.

JAMIE. Mum...you look *amazing*.

MARGARET. Scrub up quite nice yourself.

RAY. Jamie, I'm that proud of you...

*(She gives **JAMIE** a kiss and a hug, suddenly overcome.)*

*(**HUGO** rushes onstage, flustered.)*

HUGO. Is it too late, have I missed him – oh, that's the last time I put my faith in't supertram! Jamie! Thank Kylie and Jason I caught you!

JAMIE. Hugo! What are you doing here?

HUGO. I come to give you this, lad. No boy's prom dress is complete without a corsage.

*(He takes out a corsage and pins it on **JAMIE**'s wrist.)*

JAMIE. Thanks Hugo.

MARGARET. Go on then – get yourself inside.

*(**JAMIE** looks at the three of them, smiling.)*

JAMIE. Look at us...

MARGARET. Go on. This is your moment.

MISS HEDGE. Jamie New! What the hell do you think you're playing at!

*(**MISS HEDGE** comes storming out of the school, towards **JAMIE**.)*

I told you – you would not be welcome dressed like that!

JAMIE. You told me not to come as Mimi Me, Miss. And I haven't. This is just Jamie. In a dress.

MISS HEDGE. How can you think wearing a dress – *any* sort of dress – is acceptable! I have to make a stand – can't you see that?! No Jamie – you're not coming to this prom!

*(**MARGARET** goes to say something – but **RAY** stops her, 'Let him deal with this.')*

*(All eyes on **JAMIE**...who smiles, and shrugs.)*

JAMIE. Alright. Fine, fine. I don't want to spoil anyone's fun. I love me dress, and me heels. I've already got everything I wanted, so it's fine. I'll go home now. Have fun Pritti.

(*Pause.* **PRITTI** *stares at him. Then:*)

PRITTI. ARE YOU CHUFFING KIDDING ME!!! After all this!

BECCA. What's going on?

BEX. Pritti said 'chuff'.

BECCA. No! Never!

PRITTI. She won't let Jamie in cos he's wearing a dress.

MISS HEDGE. This event has a dress code.

BEX. (*Pulls out invite, reads.*) Dress code says – 'Promfabulous'. (*Points to* **JAMIE**.) Promfabulous!

MISS HEDGE. There's been complaints.

BECCA. From who?

MISS HEDGE. I can't say. A parent.

BECCA. Oh, it was Dean's dad wan't it!

(**FATIMAH** *reappears, wearing a new hijab.*)

FATIMAH. What's happening?

BECCA. She won't let Jamie in.

BEX. And Pritti said chuff.

FATIMAH. No! Never!

CY. Listen, that in't fair.

SAYID. Let him in Miss – what's the problem?

MICKEY. He's really brave. I couldn't pull that off.

LEVI. I tweeted his picture and got twelve likes. That's better than me gecko.

VICKI. Look, just let Jamie in – please!

MISS HEDGE. Ladies and Gentlemen – the doors to the Prom Hall are now open – everybody in!

BEX. No! Not without Jamie!

BECCA. He don't go in – we don't go in.

MISS HEDGE. Fine, well enjoy your prom in the car park Becca and Bex! The rest of you – inside! I said – *everybody in*!

PRITTI. No! Everybody out! Jamie! Jamie!

> *(She starts the chant – and suddenly they're all joining in [except* **DEAN** *and* **MISS HEDGE***].)*

– Jamie! Jamie! Jamie!

MISS HEDGE. Quiet! Quiet! QUIET!!!!

> *(But it's* **JAMIE** *who gestures them to hush.)*

JAMIE. Honestly, you're mad, all of you! And I can't tell you what this means to me. But this is your special night, it's not mine. You said to keep it real Miss, and I have. Prom – it's a fairy tale. But *this* – me like this – *is* real.

> *(He goes to leave.)*

MISS HEDGE. Jamie –

> *(She doesn't know what she's going to say – but suddenly she feels the need to stop him. She can't just leave it like this.* **JAMIE** *turns, and stares at* **MISS HEDGE.** **MISS HEDGE** *stares at* **JAMIE.***)*

> *(And in that moment, she feels the world changing around her.)*

...Go in.

> *(The* **KIDS** *give out a great cheer!* **JAMIE** *smiles at* **MISS HEDGE.***)*

JAMIE. Nice shoes Miss.

> *(**MISS HEDGE** *looks* **JAMIE** *up and down.)*

MISS HEDGE. Nice shoes Jamie.

> *(**BEX** *and* **BECCA** *rush over to* **MISS HEDGE** *– and lead her towards the Prom Hall.)*

BECCA. Come on Miss, are you gonna show us your moves?

BEX. Yeah, show us how they danced in black and white.

> *(The* **KIDS** *explode with excited cheers and whoops – running through the door and into the Prom Hall.)*

HUGO. Right, come on you two – Jamie, I'm evacuating them, go forth and be fabulous!

MARGARET. Hugo, are you going into town?

HUGO. Yes. Why?

MARGARET. We're all dressed up aren't we? Come on – it's not only the kids who can have fun.

RAY. Margaret New! I could kiss you!

MARGARET. Well if I don't meet anyone nice you'll have to.

RAY. Oh come here you gorgeous piece!

> (**MARGARET** *giggles, and she and* **RAY** *run off.* **HUGO** *follows them, leaving* **JAMIE** *alone with* **PRITTI**.)

JAMIE. Pritti! Get you! Leading the revolution!

PRITTI. I know. I think you're rubbing off. You're like a superhero.

JAMIE. I'm not a superhero. I'm just a boy in a dress.

PRITTI. You will dance with me, won't you?

JAMIE. Oh Pritti, you and me – we'll be dancing forever. I'll see you inside.

> (**PRITTI** *kisses* **JAMIE** *on the cheek and runs in, leaving* **JAMIE** *alone. He takes one last look around the empty car park – and then heads towards the doors, towards the sound of the party inside.)*
>
> *(Then, he pauses.)*

Aren't you coming in then?

> *(Pause. And then –* **DEAN** *emerges from behind some bins.)*

DEAN. Jog on.

JAMIE. So you know what it's like now – being the odd one out.

DEAN. Screw you, Jamie.

> *(He goes to leave.)*

JAMIE. Oh come on Dean – what's the point? We're never going to see each other again, not after tonight, so just come in, have a dance. Why not do one nice thing before it's all over?

(*DEAN stops, looks at him.*)

DEAN. Is she right? She's right, in't she?

JAMIE. Who?

DEAN. Your little friend. Big fish, small pond, you think that's me?

JAMIE. Don't matter what I think.

DEAN. Cos one day, we *will* meet again, sod's law innit Jamie, and I'll be doing some crap job, if I'm lucky – and you'll walk past me. And you won't even recognise me.

JAMIE. How could I not recognise you? You're Dean Paxton.

(*He smiles – and* **DEAN** *smiles back for the first time.*)

Come on, I'll even let you have a dance with me.
(*Stage whisper.*) *Turns out I'm pretty popular at the moment, it could help with your street cred.* Go on: be a man and take my hand.

(*Pause.*)

DEAN. I'm not gay.

JAMIE. That's alright. I'm not really a girl either. Nobody's perfect.

(*He walks forward, holds his hand out to* **DEAN.**)

So Dean, how about it, for old time's sake. One last dance?

(*The music is playing loud and clear from inside.* **DEAN** *thinks, then walks forward and takes* **JAMIE**'*s hand.*)

No, Dean – *I'll* lead.

(*Blackout.*)

11. Jamie's Street

[MUSIC NO. 17 'FINALE']

(A row of terraced houses, all exteriors with their front yards, gates and red brick yard walls – Jamie's house at the far end.)

*(**SANDRA BOLLOCK** enters in a show-stopping frock, with **TRAY SOPHISTICAY** and **LAIKA VIRGIN** sashaying in behind her.)*

TRAY SOPHISTICAY.

SO THAT'S OUR STORY

BUT WHAT'S THE LESSON?

WELL VICT'RY COMES TO THOSE THAT PUT A DRESS ON!

LAIKA VIRGIN.

BE INDIVIDUAL

DON'T ACT SO SAMEY

AND DON'T MESS WITH A BOY WHOSE NAME IS JAMIE!

SANDRA BOLLOCK.

SO IF YOU'RE WITH US

WE'LL ALL BE WINNING

LET'S GET THE DJ DOWN AND SET THE RECORD SPINNING

DRAG QUEENS.

GO RAISE THE ROOF UP

NO, EVEN HIGHER!

IT'S TIME TO PARTY –

PRITTI.

GIRLS, YOU'RE PREACHING TO THE CHOIR!

*(She leads all the other **KIDS**, including **DEAN**, onto the stage, singing like a school choir.)*

SOPRANO & TENOR.	ALTO & BASS.
EV'RYBODY'S TALKING	
	'BOUT
TALKING	
	'BOUT

SOPRANO & TENOR.	ALTO & BASS.
TALKING	
	'BOUT
CHAT CHAT CHAT	
	RAH RAH RAH
BUZZ BUZZ BUZZ	
	BLAH BLAH BLAH
EV'RY	
	BODY'S
RHUBARB	
	RHUBARB
PSS PSS	
	BUZZ BUZZ
SHH SHH	
	BUZZ BUZZ
GAB GAB	
	GOB GOB
YAP YAP	
	YAK YAK
BAA	
	BAA
MOO	
	MOO
OINK	
QUACK!	QUACK!

GROUP 1.	GROUPS 3 & 4.
EV'RYBODY'S TALKING BOUT JAMIE	EV'RYBODY'S TALKING BOUT THE BOY WHO CAME OUT THEN CAME OUT

GROUP 1.	GROUP 2.	GROUPS 3 & 4.	
EV'RYBODY'S TALKING BOUT JAMIE HEE HEE	TALKING BOUT THE BOY SO NICE HE CAME OUT TWICE	THE BOY SO NICE HE CAME OUT TWICE THEN FLEW TOO HIGH AND PAID THE PRICE	**LAIKA.**
BURNED, HE BURNED, HE BURNED UNTIL HE LEARNED	JAMIE, JAMIE	ONCE HE'D BURNED, THE LESSON LEARNED WAS THAT YOUR SPOTLIGHT MUST BE EARNED	JAMIE, JAMIE

COMPANY.

ESPECIALLY WHEN YOUR HE BECOMES A SHE-SHE-SHE-SHE-SHE

EV'RYBODY'S TALKING 'BOUT

> *(Variously.)*

JAY-AY-AY-AY-AY-AY-AY-AY-MIE!

OH

OH

AH

AH

> (**LOCO CHANELLE** *makes a grand entrance into the party:*)

LOCO CHANELLE.

ONCE IN A LIFETIME

THERE WILL RISE A HERO

WHOSE APPROACHING FOOTSTEPS

WILL CAUSE THE EARTH TO QUAKE!

LOCO CHANELLE.
> ONCE IN A LIFETIME
> THEY'LL BAPTISE A HERO
> IN THE BLOOD HE LEFT IN HIS WAKE!
> THE LEGEND OF JAMIE NEW!

MARGARET. *(Inside house.)* Jamie!

> *(Beat.)*

Jamie!

> *(Beat.)*

JAMIE!!!

JAMIE. *(Inside house.)* I know, I'm coming!

MARGARET. *(Inside house.)* You've got to put it out before the lorry comes!

JAMIE. *(Inside house.)* I know! I'm doing it!

MARGARET. *(Inside house.)* Well shake a leg!

> *(The front door opens – and a long-stockinged leg with a killer pair of heels at the foot slowly emerges – followed by the rest of* **JAMIE** *as he exits into the yard, dragged up to the nines, putting the bins out, dragging the wheelie bin behind him as he goes.)*

JAMIE. I am! I'm shaking it for all of us!

> *(Everyone joins in, singing together as one.)*

ALL.
> OUT OF THE DARKNESS

BEX & VICKI.
> A-WOO-HOO

ALL.
> INTO THE SPOTLIGHT

BEX & VICKI.
> A-WOO-HOO

ALL.
> THERE IS A NEW STAR

BEX & VICKI.
> A-WOO-HOO

ALL.
SHINING SO BRIGHT
BEX & VICKI.
A-WOO-HOO
ALL.
OUT OF THE DARKNESS
BEX& VICKI.
A-WOO-HOO
ALL.
INTO THE SPOTLIGHT
BEX & VICKI.
A-WOO-HOO
ALL.
THERE IS A NEW STAR
BEX & VICKI.
A-WOO-HOO
ALL.
SHINING SO BRIGHT
BEX & VICKI.
A-WOO-HOO

ENSEMBLE.
IN THIS PLACE WHERE
WE BELONG

BEX & VICKI.
A-WOO-HOO

ENSEMBLE.
IN THIS PLACE WHERE
WE BELONG

BEX & VICKI.
A-WOO-HOO

ENSEMBLE.
IN THIS PLACE WHERE
WE BELONG

BECCA, FATIMAH, PRITTI, CY, LEVI & SAYID
OUT OF THE DARKNESS INTO
THE SPOTLIGHT

BECCA, FATIMAH, PRITTI, CY, LEVI & SAYID
THERE IS A NEW STAR
SHINING SO BRIGHT

BECCA, FATIMAH, PRITTI, CY, LEVI & SAYID
OUT OF THE DARKNESS INTO
THE SPOTLIGHT

BEX & VICKI.

A-WOO-HOO

ENSEMBLE.

IN THIS PLACE WHERE
WE BELONG

BECCA, FATIMAH, PRITTI, CY, LEVI & SAYID

THERE IS A NEW STAR
SHINING SO BRIGHT

BEX & VICKI.

A-WOO-HOO

ALL.

OUT OF THE DARKNESS

BEX & VICKI.

A-WOO-HOO

ALL.

INTO THE SPOTLIGHT

BEX & VICKI.

A-WOO-HOO

ALL.

THERE IS A NEW STAR

BEX & VICKI.

A-WOO-HOO

ALL.

SHINING SO BRIGHT

BEX & VICKI.

A-WOO-HOO

ALL.

OUT OF THE DARKNESS

BEX& VICKI.

A-WOO-HOO

ALL.

INTO THE SPOTLIGHT

BEX & VICKI.

A-WOO-HOO

ALL.

THERE IS A NEW STAR

BEX & VICKI.

A-WOO-HOO

ALL.

SHINING SO BRIGHT

IN THIS PLACE WHERE WE BELONG
IN THIS PLACE WHERE WE BELONG
IN THIS PLACE WHERE WE BELONG
IN THIS PLACE WHERE WE BELONG

(**JAMIE**, *head held high, dancing for joy, as the lights fade slowly down around him – and to black.*)

[MUSIC NO. 18 'ENCORE: OUT OF THE DARKNESS (A PLACE WHERE WE BELONG)']

JAMIE.

WELL YOU'VE COME PRETTY FAR
BUT YOU KNOW WHERE YOU ARE
YOU'RE HOME

AND THE FRIENDS THAT YOU CHOOSE
WANT TO WALK IN YOUR SHOES
YOU'RE HOME

YOU AND ME GOT A SONG THAT WE'RE SINGING
YOU AND ME GOT A DRUM THAT WE'RE DRUMMING
LISTEN UP TO THE CHANGES WE'RE RINGING
NOTHING'S GOING TO STOP US FROM COMING

ENSEMBLE.	**MISS HEDGE, VICKI, PRITTI, DEAN, MICKEY & SAYID.**
OUT OF THE DARKNESS	OO-WOO HOO
INTO THE SPOTLIGHT	OO-WOO HOO
THERE IS A NEW STAR	OO-WOO HOO
SHINING SO BRIGHT	OO-WOO HOO
OUT OF THE DARKNESS	OO-WOO HOO
INTO THE SPOTLIGHT	OO-WOO HOO
THERE IS A NEW STAR	OO-WOO HOO
SHINING SO BRIGHT	

ALL.

> THERE'S A PLACE WHERE WE BELONG
> THERE'S A PLACE WHERE WE BELONG
> AND YOU'LL HEAR US SING OUR SONG
> IN THIS PLACE WHERE WE BELONG
>
> OUT OF THE DARKNESS
> INTO THE SPOTLIGHT
> THERE IS A NEW STAR
> SHINING SO BRIGHT
> OUT OF THE DARKNESS
> INTO THE SPOTLIGHT
> FOUND YOUR FREEDOM
> WE'RE GONNA BE ALRIGHT

ALL (EXCEPT JAMIE).

> IN THIS PLACE WHERE WE BELONG
> IN THIS PLACE WHERE WE BELONG

ALL.

> IN THIS PLACE WHERE WE BELONG

JAMIE.	**ENSEMBLE.**
IN THIS PLACE WHERE WE BELONG	HMM

[MUSIC NO. 19 'EXIT MUSIC']

The End

GLOSSARY

Author's Notes

Notherners: *someone who lives in the north of England.*

Page 1

Year 11: *final year of secondary school in the UK.*

Tatty: *worn and shabby.*

Gobby: *talking too loudly in a blunt way.*

Page 3

Boots: *a UK high street chemist.*

Quorn: *a brand of vegetarian meat alternative.*

Hoots of derision: *when someone or something is laughed at and considered of no value.*

Rubbish: *very bad; useless.*

Abattoir: *a slaughterhouse.*

Page 4

Away with the fairies: *lost in a daydream.*

Page 5

Au Revoir (French): *goodbye until we meet again.*

Page 13

Footballers: *Soccer players.*

Revision timetables: *timetable used for revising for exams.*

Nail varnish: *nail polish.*

Page 14

Council Estate: *low-income social housing.*

From't: *a Sheffieldism, meaning 'from the'.*

Fighting Cock: *the name of a pub.*

Meat raffle: *as it sounds, a raffle (lottery) where the prizes are meat.*

20p: *twenty pence.*

Mince: *ground meat.*

Page 15

N'owt: *nothing.*

In't yard: *in the yard.*

Petal: *term of endearment.*

Lah-de-dah: *fancy, higher class.*

Bloody: *used to express surprise or anger.*

Page 16

Penelope Pitstop: *animated character who drives a racing car, The Compact Pussycat.*

Twenty quid: *twenty pounds, £20.*

I'nt: *abbreviation of isn't.*

Page 17

Chuff: *British slang replacement for harsher swear word. Usuall seen as a more playful term.*

Meadow Hall: *shopping centre/mall in Sheffield.*

Page 23

Lush: *great*

Canal Street: *famous street in the centre of Manchester's Gay Village.*

Daft: *silly.*

GBF: *Gay Best Friend.*

Page 24

Carol Vorderman: *glamorous TV presenter known for her maths skills.*

Willies: *slang for penis, less rude.*

On't: *abbreviation of on it.*

Parson Cross: *area in Sheffield.*

Page 25

Bezzy mates: *best friends.*

Page 26

Swotty: *a swot, someone who works hard in school.*

Speccy: *wears spectacles.*

Emmeline Pankhurst: *English political activist who organized the suffragette movement which helped women win the right to vote.*

Bent: *meaning gay, queer.*

Get Stuffed: *telling someone to go away.*

Povvo: *poor.*

Page 29

Ice cream, in a tiny tub, with a built in spoon: *Ice creams sold during the interval in British theatres often come with a spoon in the lid.*

Page 30

Frock: a *dress.*

Page 31

OTT: *Over The Top*

Day-glow colours: *bright, neon colours.*

Till: *cash register.*

Page 32

Ossifying: *to become rigid.*

Page 34

Ballbags: *slang for scrotum*

Page 35

Pet: *a typical and affectionate way to end a greeting in the North East of England.*

Page 36

Southey Green: *a social housing project in Sheffield.*

Page 38

Finchley: *a borough of London. There is, sadly, no Novotel in Finchley.*

Page 41

The Social: *social club; a venue for entertainment and drinking, usually in a working class area.*

Page 42

Poppet: *affectionate name used for a small child or sweetheart.*

T'other: *abbreviation of the other.*

Page 45

Wednesday: *Sheffield Wednesday, the local soccer team.*

Ow't: *abbreviation of anything.*

Page 49

Cooee: *used to attract attention.*

Ey up: *'hello' or 'how are you'*

Pound Shop: *discount store.*

Lippie: *lipstick.*

Aldi: *budget supermarket chain.*

After Sevens: *a play on After Eights, a box of chocolate covered mints.*

Page 50

Brown sauce: *a popular British condiment, often used alongside, or instead of, ketchup.*

Own brand: *unbranded, a supermarket's own brand.*

Daddies: *a brand of brown sauce.*

Page 51

Ruddy do it: *go on and do it.*

Page 55

Go to Cambridge: *go to study at the prestigious Cambridge University.*

Page 56

Leggie: *a leg up.*

Arse: *ass.*

Page 58

The loo: *toilet/bathroom.*

Lichtenstein: *an American artist.*

Tracey Emin: *a British artist.*

Grayson Perry: *a British artist.*

Page 59

Yoko Ono: *Singer, married to Beatle John Lennon.*

Duchamp: *An French artist.*

Half a dead cow in a tank: *refers to artist Damien Hirst's artwork.*

Page 63

An't I: *abbreviation of aren't I.*

Minger: *insulting term to call someone unattractive.*

Ta-ra: *good-bye.*

Page 64

ASDA: *British supermarket.*

Well jell: *very jealous.*

Dun't he: *doesn't he.*

Page 65

Cistern flushing: *toilet flushing.*

Page 66

Nips: *nipples.*

Page 76

Knickers: *women's underwear.*

Page 83

Fit: *attractive.*

Now't special: *nothing special.*

Page 84

Murs Bar, Kat-Kit, Twox, Maltoosers: *a play on the names of famous UK chocolate bars – Mars Bar, Kit-Kat, Twix, Maltesers (Whoppers).*

Cuppa?: *Would you like a cup of tea?*

Pull in a drag club: *pick up a man in a drag club.*

Page 85

Stop whittlin' woman: *stop complaining woman.*

The Black Bull: *the name of a pub.*

G'yaw: *stop going on, stop having a go at me.*

Page 97
  Your'sen: *yourself.*

Page 111
  Car park: *parking lot.*

Page 112
  Looks lush on you: *looks great on you.*

Page 114
  Nailed you: *put you in your place.*

Page 115
  Oh Kiddah: *punjabi word for how u doin.*

  Masha Allah: *punjabi words used to express a feeling of beauty.*

  Auntie-Ji: *punjabi word – a respectful name and form of address given to an older woman.*

Page 116
  Supertram: *tram service in Sheffield.*

  Kylie and Jason: *Kylie Minogue and Jason Donovan, famous as a pop duo in the 80s and much beloved by the UK gay community.*

Page 120
  Sod's law: *used to refer to the humorous statement that if something can go wrong then it will go wrong.*

Page 124
  Lorry: *the rubbish collection van.*
  Shake a leg: *a phrase meaning 'go on and do it'.*
  Putting the bins out: *putting the rubbish/trash out.*

  Wheelie bin: *domestic refuse bin on wheels, used in most British homes.*

Milton Keynes UK
Ingram Content Group UK Ltd.
UKHW020721121023
430452UK00012B/301